Mr Right and other Mongrels

Monique McDonell

Published by Redfish Publishing

Copyright 2012. Monique McDonell

Cover by Lisa Kelly

All characters in this book are fiction and figments of the author's imagination.

www.moniquemcdonell.com.au

Thank You

To Ross and Charlotte who always believe in me.

CHAPTER ONE

First of all there is something you need to know about me. Dogs and I do not get along.

It's not that I don't like them, exactly. In theory, I love them.

In reality I have a full-blown hysterical dog phobia.

Ok now. Wait. Don't just decide you dislike me based on that.

I know how dog people are. They simply don't like people who don't like dogs, but honestly it just isn't that simple. That is like saying you hate all Mormons when that's not possible and really how many do you actually know?

The thing is when I was a child there were a few dog-related incidents that led to the dogs charging at me with teeth bared. Once when I was about eight I was forced to throw myself in front of a two-year-old and offer my leg as a snack to a Doberman, so that the dog wouldn't rip into the smaller child's face. Now objectively I know that was just bad luck and I came across the wrong dog. But honestly, it wasn't just the once…anyway, more about that later.

It's because of the dog phobia that I first met Edward Green, also known as Teddy Green, television celebrity and garden guru, but of course I didn't know that at the time.

I was walking along a nice tree-lined street in Sydney's lush eastern suburbs minding my own business. I'd been shopping with my friends Lisa and Caroline in Paddington and I'd parked back in Woollahra to save myself a cab-fare home.

Ordinarily I would still have been sitting in the pub with the girls but I had a family event to get to. We don't have functions or dinners in our family, everything is an event.

OK, so I start walking along the street and out bounds an over-excited Old-English Sheepdog who decides to lunge at me...don't laugh because I know they are considered really cute but they are also very big, quite stupid and not very good at listening to an hysterical woman who is screaming.

"Please go away! Good dog. Go home! Go home."

So in the absence of anyone else on the street, and anyone who has walked the streets of Woollahra on a Saturday afternoon knows how rare that is, I found myself climbing into the back of a Ute to get away from the dog. After 10 minutes of barking and jumping and panting the dog lay down behind the vehicle on the warm asphalt and fell asleep, thus blocking my exit.

Meanwhile I was left standing in the flat bed of the ute wondering how I could make my escape. To add to my stress every so often the dog would twitch as if he was in the middle of a rather exciting dream or scratch himself behind the ear. As I was trying to work out what to do to make my escape, help arrived in the form of a cute, brown-haired guy who just happened to be Mr Teddy Green, national icon and ute owner.

He sauntered out of the front gate of a terrace house, listening to his iPod, and came from the front of the car and got in. Why he didn't see me I have no idea. He was about to drive off when I began banging furiously on the rear window of the cabin. Eventually the vibrations and noise got his attention and he climbed out.

"Uhmmmmm Hello... You're in my ute." Very articulate.

"Yes, this dog chased me in here and I have a bit of a dog phobia and..." Then I burst into tears. Now I must tell you that at this time I didn't know who he was...I don't own a TV...so I didn't know that I should have been feeling even more embarrassed and pathetic than I was.

Just then the dog woke up and leapt at Mr Green.

"This is the dog you are scared of?" he looked quite incredulous. He ruffled its fur and tickled it behind the ears.

"I'm scared of all dogs...but right now, yes THIS is the dog." I was also searching in my bag for a tissue.

"Oh."

"If you just move it away then I can get out of your truck and go home. It got out of that gate," I pointed and indicated.

So he walked the dog back and shut the gate, the same gate Teddy had just come through and I climbed down. I patted my eyes and was thankful that at least, if nothing else that day had gone right, I had worn waterproof mascara.

He swaggered back and smiled.

"Thanks so much. Sorry if I held you up." I said as I started to walk off.

"Does this happen to you often?" he asked

"The dog part or the ute part?"

"Both I guess."

"The dog part is common. The ute part is an embarrassing new low. Thanks for rescuing me."

And that's how it all began.

***

My building is quite literally 'my building'. The shop is downstairs and I live upstairs. It's the way it's always been. Well, not always but since I was 16.

Most people look at shops and they know there is room above but I guess they never really think about what is up there. Lots of people live above shops the world over and even in big cities like Sydney, it's not really that uncommon, but most people I know think it's a quirky choice.

I live in Manly, a beachside suburb that is a tourist hotspot. It's full of backpackers and English tourists making the most of the strong pound.

The bookshop I run is down stairs and then the apartment is above. It's not a huge apartment but it's totally perfect for me. It has wonderful old sash windows and a little tiny Juliet balcony in the back that over-looks an alley...and at the front there is the big metal shopfront awning, which affords me a ton of privacy from the street below. I recently had it painted green because it was pretty scratched and it was reflecting way too much sun back into my bedroom. A girl needs to be able to sleep in, now doesn't she?

My friends think I should move. You know how in the modern age everyone is very big on the separation of his or her home life and work life. Compartmentalising is the phrase they use. Otherwise apparently there can be a blurring of the boundaries.

I totally love the blurring of the boundaries. For example I have these fantastic traditional silk PJs that I got in Chinatown. So sometimes if I wake up with a bad hangover and I am expecting people in the shop for a delivery or to get a pick-up then I just pin a flower in my hair, slide on some cute shoes, gargle with Listerine and go down and open up with my cup of tea in hand. How perfect is that? That is a very positive blurring of boundaries.

I love that Mrs Tang from the clothing alteration shop starts to panic if the shop isn't open at 10.15am. I love that Cherie from the Beauticians comes and does my nails if we are both having a slow Monday. I love that Joe from the coffee shop at the end of the arcade wanders by with treats and cups of coffee for me when he is feeling generous or flirty, or his wife Connie comes by with pictures of the grandkids, or the grandkids themselves. How nice is that to have such a great community around you?

The girls say it is a hangover from my hippy roots. That need for a community. I don't think so. I think everyone has the same need deep down. I tell them often that they are just in high-powered denial.

It isn't that I don't get their point. Sometimes when I have tax stuff to do or business is a bit slow, well then I do wish I could walk out the front door and really and truly leave it all behind. Having said that I know my brain would be just as active wherever I was and the benefits so outweigh the negatives for me.

Anyway, so it was Sunday afternoon and I was upstairs because Lucie was in the shop and it wasn't far from closing and I was just over the whole weekend and I wasn't needed anyway.

So I had just put on my very daggy tracksuit and some slippers. My tracksuit was not one of the gelato coloured velour ones the yummy-mummies strut down Manly beach in after dropping the children at school (although don't tell my friends but I do have a beautiful aquamarine one I wear very occasionally.) No, the tracksuit in question was over 10 years old and consisted of very grubby navy-blue Sydney University sweatshirt and old fashioned grey pants. It's hideous but gloriously comfortable.

So the kettle was just on when I heard a knock at the door and I open it because I figured it was Lucie. Instead I found a good-looking and vaguely familiar guy standing there. I knew I had met him, but honestly I could not place exactly where.

"Hi!" he said.

"Hi. Can I help you?" I asked.

It then dawned upon him that I basically had no idea who he was or what he was doing here.

"Umm, well hi. We met yesterday when you were in the back of my ute."

So then it came rushing back in a wave of total embarrassment. I couldn't remember him because, in a way only the deeply traumatised can, I had totally blocked out his details. Of course I knew it was a good-looking guy who had rescued me but beyond that all my memory revealed is an outline. The big hairy dog however remained crystal clear. People who have never experienced that kind of humiliation can't really understand the heady mix of self-consciousness and humiliation and how it can mess with one's head.

"Oh, yes. Well, look I am so sorry about that."

"I just stopped by because you dropped your wallet. I'm surprised you haven't noticed." He said as he held out his hand, "By the way I'm Teddy Green."

"Oh. Did I?" I was very flustered by now. "Look, come in. Sorry I look dreadful, the house is a mess, but come in…" Then as I offered my own hand I took the opportunity to see who I was actually talking to and noticed he was Country Road catalogue perfect. Perfect blue pants and a perfect checked shirt, perfect loafers, even. He was the whole nine yards.

"I didn't mean to barge in," he said stepping through the door, "I didn't find it till this afternoon, it was hidden beneath a tool box. I was up at Newport and I figured it was on the way back through, so I thought I'd drop it off. I left you a message."

I looked around and saw my machine was bipping. And then the kettle whistled.

"Oh excuse me a moment," I said heading for the kitchen. He followed me in and shut the door. "Would you like a cup of tea? I was just about to have one."

"Sure". He called out as I headed down the hall. "I love your place."

"Oh you are very polite, aren't you? Sorry, it's a bit of a mess right now."

The truth was my place really was very nice in an eclectic kind of way. And it was equally true that is was a total mess. There was a pile of books here, a washing basket of stuff there. The coffee table was barely visible under the weekend paper.

"Well, that's true." He smiled and there were the perfect teeth again. "But I can tell that deep down it's a great place."

"Yeah, about two feet deep down." We both laughed.

"Listen, my name is Allegra Johnson."

"I know. I have your wallet." Of course, my wallet has my license in it and that was how he knew where to find me.

"Oh yes. Thanks for bringing it back. That was really very kind."

"You're welcome. Can I ask how you can be wallet-less for over 24 hours and simply not know?"

"Good question, I guess, although not if you knew me. I pay cash for everything. No credit cards. And I keep stashes of cash in every bag – don't rob me, OK?"

"OK."

"So I would have noticed in a day or so…or if I'd been pulled over I guess."

"Does that happen often?" he looked very concerned. As if I was a driving deviant or something.

"Well if you saw my car it would make more sense. Plus my brother-in-law is a local cop. I know all his mates…sometimes they pull me over for sport."

"Oh, fair enough." He was smiling now.

"Anyway and this weekend hasn't been a great one. You know that because you were there for one of the better moments…."

"That was a `better' moment?" He interrupted.

"Oh totally one of the good ones. So needless to say my ability to create order and do things like find my wallet has been somewhat limited." I stopped to sip my tea. "Anyway, you brought my wallet back so there is hope for the world. And by the way, I know you told me but I didn't catch your name."

"Teddy Green."

And that was how I met Teddy Green for the second time.

We sat there quietly sipping our tea.

My phone rang, and I excused myself. It was Lucie.

"Hey Ally, I saw some dude come up there. Are you OK?"

I knew she wanted the goss. To know me was to know that dudes like the one sitting in my kitchen having an English Breakfast tea don't cross my doorway often. And honestly as far as I knew they didn't cross Lucie's doorway very often either, so if the shoe had been on the other foot I would have been calling too.

"Yeah fine, is it closing time."?

"Yep."

"OK see you Wednesday."

"You are really not going to tell me anything."

"That's right." I answered evenly.

"Arghhhhhh, Allegra." She moaned as she hung up.

I went back to the kitchen and he was flicking through an old Manly daily that was on the table.

"Neighbour?"

"From my shop downstairs."

"You have a shop?" He seemed a little *too* surprised for my liking, but then I was sounding, acting and looking like a total loser, so I had to cut him some slack.

"Hard though that may be to believe, yes I do. A bookshop."

"Oh sorry I didn't mean to imply that…."

"It's OK, Teddy. You would not be the first." I sighed and sipped my tea.

"So what do you do?" I asked. I thought it was polite to show some interest. "No, let me guess. Ok you own a ute and you are too neat to be a plumber or a builder."

"Thanks, I think." He smiled.

"I bet you are a landscape gardener."

"Good guess."

"Is that a fun job? It must be, all the beautiful flowers and seeing things come to life."

"Well it can be very rewarding. It's not as fun as it used to be. The industry is getting rather high pressure, but it is a good job."

I blinked. Who ever thought of gardening as high pressure? That just goes to show what I know.

"Wow, high pressure gardening. Intense."

We had both finished our tea. I thought that maybe I should offer him a reward. But how does one do that without sounding like a crackpot?

"Listen, thanks for bringing my wallet. I feel like I should do something nice for you now, especially as you also saved my life yesterday."

"I think that is a slight exaggeration…that dog would only have drooled you to death."

"EWWWW but what a way to go." I shivered. "Well I could take you out for a drink or dinner."

He looked at me. I couldn't tell what he was thinking. Probably, why is the horrible weird-looking girl hitting on me?

"I don't mean now. Just one day. I'm not hitting on you, just so you know."

He laughed. "Well that would be nice. What about Wednesday? What time do you finish up?"

"Well, Wednesday is fine. I shut the shop at 6pm. Do you want to meet me downstairs then?"

"That would be great." He stood to leave. "Allegra it has been delightful meeting you." He must have been easily delighted, I thought.

And then he left.

CHAPTER TWO

On Monday morning I rang my friend Lisa for our usual post-weekend de-brief. She told me how they, the girls, had stayed and had a few drinks in Paddington after I left them. She also told me about how she and her fiancé Greg spent Sunday discussing the seating plan for their upcoming wedding with both their sets of parents.

I told her about the horror that was my father's 50th birthday party on the Saturday night.

"It is never good Lisa, when Dad gathers the children from his three relationships together. It totally does my head in."

"Yes, how was the evil Rebecca?" That is how we refer to my eldest half sister.

"She was her usual charming self. I honestly don't know why she even turns up. I think it is just to make the evening extra crappy for the rest of us, especially Dad."

"I don't like to be unkind, but I do think you may be right about that," said Lisa. "Did your Dad have fun?"

"Oh yeah he was like that cat that swallowed the cream…only it was pot not cream he'd swallowed, as per usual."

"Wasn't that a bit awkward for the lovely Debbie and Davo the cop?"

"Ah yes, indeed it was. So as you can imagine it was the usual Johnson horror show."

"Ah well Ally, the important thing is, your Dad may be a bit of a nutter, but he does love you all." She was right about that.

***

My family tree is a gnarled old thing with branches coming off in all directions, thanks to my dear old Dad, Johno Johnson. In the early 1970s he was married to a nice girl he'd met at high school, called Marlene. He spent time working as a real estate agent and hanging at the local surf club on the weekends. He drank his beers at The Steyne and in between was hopelessly devoted to his three kids, Rebecca, Debbie and Johno Jnr.

Then along came my mother Sophia Hawkins. She was the family's 18 year old babysitter and he was smitten. My mother was a sexy cheese-cloth wearing nymph who spoke of free love, drugs and exploring your true self. Marlene only hired her as a favour to my grandmother, a decision she lived to regret.

Poor old Johno was hopelessly smitten and in a highly uncharacteristic display he left Manly and headed with my mum to northern New South Wales to hang out on a commune.

And then along came me.

Then follows a rather long and lamentable story, which involves my headstrong mother taking me and leaving him and severing all ties for good. Fast forward, and several years later he found himself living in Byron Bay with the lovely Rosie and he was again in a happy family situation with my twin half-sister and brother Stella Moon and Dylan Oak.

My Dad is no longer a hippy but it is still in his blood. Put it this way the less alternative members of the community would still think of him as one but the purists would think he was a sell out. Either way he still likes a toke at parties. And naturally his own birthday party was no exception to that rule.

It's complicated because one of my half sisters Debbie is married to a local cop and it isn't great for him to be hanging with Johno when he's stoned. The strange thing is no one loves Johno more than Dave, but it does put him in an interesting position from time to time. Dave usually goes home and relieves the babysitter about the time Johno brings out the joints.

So on the Saturday night we had all gathered for a big event that involved all three families and as many of Johno's mates as he could muster. These events are obviously a little fraught because you can't create three branches of a family tree without some tension and of course half the guests can't quite recall who is who or how we fit together so we are just all called 'Darling', especially as the night wears on.

And as he always does Johno has to pull us each aside and tell us how much he loves us and how he is sorry for the trail of debris he has left. Of course whether we feel forgiving or not we all say we are, that is, all except Rebecca - who it seems plain to everyone but Johno, has no intention of ever forgiving him.

And thus, in the tradition of an old not very groovy hippy, after talking to her, he usually picks up his guitar and starts to sing anthemic folk songs such as *Blowing in the Wind* or *Kumbayah* and that is pretty much a sign to run for your life.

Lisa has had the great pleasure of attending previous Johnson family events so she knows the drill. I filled her in a bit but there wasn't a need to really break down the details.

So naturally in the tradition of all brides-to-be everywhere, she steered the conversation back to herself.

"Anyway Allegra, are you bringing a date to the wedding? You don't have to let me know now, because we still have a month to go."

"Who would I bring?" It then occurred to me that I could ask Teddy Green. And I laughed. "Maybe I can bring Teddy".

"Who is Teddy, Ally?"

So I told her.

"Oh my God, Allegra. That's Teddy Green, TV's gardening guru."

"I doubt it. He just said he was a landscape gardener."

"That's definitely him. I bet it is. He lives in Woollahra with Louisa Lane, you know the magazine editor. And you met him in Woollahra so it must be him.

He's on *Garden Dreams, Homemakeover Magic* and *Celebrity Gardens by Surprise.* You must have recognized him."

"Lisa, you know I don't watch TV."

"Right, well, get your butt down to the newsagency, look in this week's TV Week and see if it's him. Oh my God!! I bet it is him. You are having drinks with the nation's hottest celebrity, Allegra."

"It can't be him". It couldn't be, I thought.

But of course it was.

And that was how I found out I was having drinks, but definitely not a date, with Teddy Green, Garden Guru.

***

So when Wednesday rolled around I was kind of nervous. And of course, by then, I knew who he was. There had been so many phone calls from the girls, and Lucie had been at me all day. It was making my head spin.

If I had to say, 'it's not a date, one more time I thought I would scream.

"So when a gorgeous guy meets you for a drink, when is it a date then?" quizzed Lucie over coffee that morning.

"It's a date when they are into you, or when they ask you out." That was my very reasonable answer.

"He might be into you, you know", she suggested.

How could I respond to that except by rolling my eyes and sipping my coffee? Apart from anything else, according to Lisa and TV Week, he had a girlfriend.

"Lucie, the first time I met him I was having a panic attack, and the second time he met me I was wearing a dirty tracksuit, there is no way Mr TV is into me."

"Well Allegra you never know. He did agree to have a drink with you, after all."

"It's a pity drink. I think celebrities have to do things like that so we don't all talk badly about them."

"I don't think so Allegra. It's not like you met him through the Make-a-Wish Foundation."

All I knew was that at 6pm I was to take the nation's hottest property out for a drink.

What does one wear? Obviously not one's tracksuit. The girls were all giving me advice and it was unhelpfully all conflicting. Something flirty, something understated. Bright colours. Basic black. Heels or flats?

In the end I settled on a black flowing skirt, a lavender singlet top with sequins around the neckline from Witchery, low black heels and a very cute Victoria Springs hairclip. I looked neat and presentable and clean which I think is a must as a minimum. I did at least look and feel like myself.

He turned up about twenty minutes late looking drop-dead gorgeous and a bit frazzled. His hair looked less neat and he had a vaguely distracted look about him.

"Sorry Allegra, a bit of a problem at work today."

"Oh that's OK. Everyone has those days." He was staring absently around the shop no doubt wondering what sorts of crises might befall my business from time to time.

"Shall we go?"

So I locked up the shop while he ran outside to make a phone call. As I came out I could hear him saying,

"Look Louisa, I will talk to you later. Now is not a good time." It sounded rather intimate so I tried to look busy. "I'll call you tomorrow...not tonight."

He turned around and looked guilty. Weird, I thought.

"Sorry again."

"That's fine. You could have cancelled, you know. I just wanted to say thank you, not stress you out," I said sweetly.

"Oh, Allegra, no. I have been so looking forward to this. I hope I don't seem that rude."

"Not at all. So do you want to go straight to a pub or somewhere we can grab a snack too?"

"I think food too."

OK that was interesting, he was obviously not too desperate to get away if he was committing to snacks.

As we walked down the Corso it was very strange, because people were staring at us. How bizarre was that? I didn't say anything and it was as if he honestly didn't notice.

So, as we strolled along the Corso the funniest thing happened - we ran into my stepsister, Rebecca. Now Rebecca doesn't much like me and blames me for the demise of her parents' marriage, but none of that was obvious with Teddy around. Anyway, it was amazing what hanging with a celebrity can do for your cause.

"Oh Allegra. Hi!"

"Hi Rebecca."

"How are you?"

"Same as I was on Saturday thanks" I didn't add 'when you were a horrible cow to me', tempted though I was. "And you?"

"Oh great, just great. Aren't you going to introduce me to your friend?" Shit, could she be more obvious?

"Oh yes, Teddy. My sister Rebecca."

"Nice to meet you Rebecca. Do you all live locally too?"

"Well my sister and brother do, and Allegra"

"Isn't Allegra your sister too?" He asked quizzically.

"She is only my half sister" she replied spitting the word half out like it had a bad taste about it.

"Well Rebecca we are in rather a hurry…"

"Yes well, me too. See you then." And she strode off with force. She always walked like she was going into battle.

"She seemed pleasant," he said politely.

"Did she? Well she isn't at all pleasant." I probably sounded like a total bitch. "Let's go to Leaping Waves."

"OK."

We walked on in silence.

"Do you have brothers and sisters Teddy?" He didn't answer. "Sorry I didn't mean to pry."

"No, you're fine. I have three brothers."

We reached the restaurant. It was only a block from the Corso and across from the beach. They have nice outside tables and a cute banquette along the inside window. Teddy seemed to visibly relax once we sat down.

We sat on the banquette. Well I did, Teddy sat opposite me. We ordered a couple of beers and bar snacks. I am not really a beer drinker but it seemed like the right drink.

"So have you been attacked by any dogs this week?" he asked.

"Thankfully, no. It's been better. Actually it happens less often than you might expect."

"Well that's good. Let's have a toast. To your safety."

"And to your chivalry." I sounded like a loser from a nineteenth century novel. I didn't care though. It's funny how when you know the person you are with has no interest in you whatsoever, you simply relax.

"Chivalry. Not a word used too often these days."

"That's because there isn't enough of it on display."

"You don't think so?"

"Well maybe it's just my life, but I don't see much evidence I'd have to say."

"That seems a shame. You seem like a damsel who might often find herself in distress." Did I now? I must have glared because he added "In a good way."

"Thanks. I think."

"So tell me Teddy. Where do you live?"

"Oh, well, I am moving just now. From Woollahra to Lavender Bay"

"Oh, how is that going?"

"Great. I've just finished renovating a place. You should come and see it. I am having a housewarming party this Saturday night. I'd love it if you'd come."

"Really?"

"Sure, why not?"

"I don't know how much I'd have in common with all those landscape gardeners." I said sweetly.

"I guess you have figured out I have other parts of my job too huh?"

"Yep."

"I honestly couldn't believe you had no idea. I don't mean to sound arrogant."

"That's fine. Look I don't own a TV so honestly I was clueless as to who you were."

"Wow! No TV. That's fantastic."

"Well sure, but not very good for your business," I offered.

"True. But it's great. You must be the first person I met in the past two or three years who didn't recognise me. It was kind of nice."

"Well I'll have to take your word for that. As I'm not recognised much anywhere."

Well ironically just then someone I knew waved at me from the street. It was my Nanna's old neighbour Len, out for his evening walk.

"Well I think you're recognised around here. That's the second time tonight."

"Yes but don't take me further than a kilometre in any direction. It's not quite the same, anyway, as those people do actually know me."

"Yes, well, that would be the major difference." He finished off his Crown Lager.

"Do you want another beer?" I expected he'd make a polite excuse to leave but he didn't.

"Sure. But you've hardly touched yours."

"Do you want the truth?"

"Always," he said earnestly, but half joking.

"I really don't like beer. I just couldn't decide what to have. But maybe I'll get a wine instead." We both laughed.

"I really like you Allegra. I like your honesty."

So we sat there and chatted about dog phobias and the surf and my dislike of beer and his overwhelming love of it after a hot day at work. And we had another drink and he refused to let me pay even though I was the one who had invited him out.

"Well you can pay next time." So it seemed there would be a next time.

He walked me back to the store as the sun was setting.

"How long have you lived here?" he asked

"About 10 years, now, I guess."

"Ten years! You must have been young."

"Yeah, sixteen."

"It's a great spot."

"Yeah, it is. Well it's great for me. It's home."

And then we were there.

He pulled out his card and wrote his home number and address on it under the business details.

"I insist you come to my party. And you can bring a friend or boyfriend or whatever."

"Well I don't have a boyfriend," Idiot Allegra, idiot. "But I have tons of friends." Now that just sounded pathetic. "Look, I'll try and make it."

"Please come, Allegra" he said and he leant in and kissed my cheek. "It would make my night." And he looked right into my eyes and honest to God, I thought I would faint.

And then he walked off

"See you Saturday", he called over his shoulder.

CHAPTER THREE

I talked Lucie into coming with me to the party. None of the other girls could come on short notice and there was no way I would be going it alone.

I am really not that great at parties even at the best of times. The best of times is when you really know the person having the party and you feel like it's appropriate to be attending. An even better party is when you also know the majority of the people going and then you can relax and just be yourself.

A party where the only person you know is the host, and in all honesty you don't even know him, or why he has invited you for that matter, this is not the ideal party.

Teddy left a message on my machine on the Friday.

On it he said;

"Hey Allegra, Teddy Green here. Thanks for the other night. I am looking forward to seeing you tomorrow night. You've got the address. 19 Dream House Lane, naff street name I know, oh yes and its casual-dress. See you then. It's anytime from 8pm." Pause. "There will be no dogs."

I decided to drive. I know from experience that a nervous Allegra at the start of a party will be an embarrassed and intoxicated Allegra about an hour in. So if I drive I can't drink, well that is the theory. And if I change my mind I can always grab a cab home.

Which is how I found myself sitting in Dream House Lane, in my ancient VW van with the lovely Lucie who looked, I must say at the risk of sounding jealous, leggy and luscious and not at all like a poor student who works in a second-hand bookshop. Apparently away from the shop Lucie is quite the vixen and she loves a long boot, a short skirt, a flash of thigh and a sparkle of sequins. Lucie's casual was infinitely sexier than mine.

I was wearing black pants, strappy shoes with medium kitten heels, a black vintage Lisa Ho top and my hair pulled back in a ponytail with a large diamante encrusted hairclip shaped like a lily. The hairclip was a new purchase for the occasion but everything else was a favourite.

A few people strolled past and entered the party. Their idea of casual was apparently even less casual than Lucie's. Some people Lucie recognised from TV. Naturally, not being a TV fan, I recognised no one.

We noted that, just like at other parties held by uni students and shop owners, guests came lugging six-packs of beer and bottles of wine, although we were fairly certain no one was bringing low-budget Passion Pop or a flagon as their contribution.

"Well Ally, we just can't sit here all night," said the wise Lucie. Lucie was actually looking forward to the party, quite unlike me. I think she was hoping to meet a few minor celebrities.

"OK Lucie. Let's get it over with." It was 9.15pm.

We grabbed our bottles, checked our lipstick and headed nervously for the front door.

The house was a very modern and ultra groovy terrace. It was designed to within an inch of its life.

The interior was a study of charcoal, grey, stark white and flashes of red. It seemed to me not at all the sort of place Teddy would have chosen, but it did seem rather like a home from TV or Vogue.

The whole downstairs area flowed into one big space, divided by petitions and open shelves with fabulous pots on them.

You could see through from the front door to a gorgeous courtyard, with built in seating and water features. I don't know much about garden design but I do know that water features seem to be taking over urban backyards across the country.

We knocked and then entered as the door was open and, as we know, that is international party protocol. I looked around for the host. There were easily over one hundred people there.

Out the side of her mouth Lucie tried to tell me subtly who various people were.

"That is Daisy Roberts from the travel program" or "there is the guy who hosts the dancing show" or "that is the building dude Bill Hughes who works on Teddy's show."

We smiled and tried to look as if we belonged and found where to deposit our bottles and get some glasses from which to drink. We were assisted by a lizard like man who managed to show us to the drinks table.

"Hi, I'm Nathan." His pasty face was oozing out of the top of his turtleneck sweater.

" I'm Allegra, this is Lucie."

"Oh do you girls work at the TV station?" He quickly poured us each a champagne as he talked. He was looking Lucie up and down, up and down.

"No, I'm a student," offered Lucie. And then she and the lizard were having quite a discussion about the rising price of university fees. He was old enough to be her father and if he went to university at all, which I doubted, he certainly did it long before the introduction of Australian university fees in the late eighties. I figured his intimate knowledge was because he probably had a couple of kids at uni already.

I excused myself and wandered off to find Teddy. I have a party policy that I find the host fast because I always stay exactly one and a half hours at parties I don't belong at and I have to make sure it looks at least that long to the host.

I made my way to the courtyard and could see he was deep in conversation with a leggy and rather sexy brunette and another man. She kept touching him in that possessive way some women do and so I decided to lean against a door and watch. Aside from anything else I couldn't work out exactly how to break into the conversation, but sometimes it is nice to just stop and get your bearings.

As a kid my mother dragged me to many parties. Invariably I didn't know too many people and she would always wander off and I would be left standing in a corner. As I got older it bothered me less and less. I still don't like parties as a result but I am no longer nervous standing alone. I have come to realise that most people are so busy worrying about their own fun or inadequacy they barely even register one lonely girl standing in the corner.

While I stood there a band started playing in the courtyard and a few people started to dance. The sexy brunette was doing that confident skinny girl dancing with her hands writhing seductively over her head. Teddy didn't really dance he kind of swayed a bit, in that self-conscious way many men do.

He was wearing black pants, exceptionally shiny black shoes and a white shirt with an almost invisible thin black stripe. He looked more urban and groovy tonight. Like he needed to match the house. He also looked less relaxed I thought, but then who doesn't look a little tense at their own party. It's a lot of pressure throwing a party.

"That's Louisa," a female voice said to me. "And I am guessing you are Allegra."

I was somewhat startled. A small woman with a severe bob was standing beside me. I hadn't heard her coming over the band.

"Ah yes I am. And you are?"

"Sorry, I'm Jane Lewis, Teddy's assistant. He told me to keep an eye out for you."

"How did you know who I was?" I was wondering how I'd been described.

"Easy. Teddy told me you were a very attractive brunette in your late twenties and your friend is a younger blonde." He had said I was attractive, oh my!

"Well, that makes sense."

"Also, I know everyone else here except you two."

"Ah the powers of deduction!" I suggested. "It's nice to meet you. I feel a bit weird about coming but Teddy was kind of insistent…"

"It's great you came. He'll be thrilled. Now if I can just get him away from her." Her voice was heavy with contempt.

"Who is she? His girlfriend?"

"She's the ex-girlfriend, honey."

So she was the Ex girlfriend! That was interesting new information to process.

"But she might just want to change her mind *again*. And I am hoping you and I don't let that happen." Jane winked at me, smiled and walked away.

How was I going to stop that from happening? Who was I anyway? I was just some crazy ditz who lost her wallet. Why was she telling me this? Too many questions so I sipped my very nice champagne. I had brought Fleur de Lys but as there had been Möet on offer who was I to say no? That would have been just plain rude.

Just then Teddy turned and saw me. He beamed that big perfect smile right to the corners of his gorgeous blue eyes.

"You made it!" He walked over and hugged me. It felt lovely and embarrassing all at once. You need to know that I am not good with public displays of affection. And especially not at crowded parties full of people I don't know.

He grabbed my hand. My breathing about stopped.

"Come let me give you a tour." And we were off leaving the stunned Louisa in our wake.

As we went through the house I noticed Lucie was still with the Lizard, but she seemed to quite like him. Weird how different people's taste can be?

"Who's my friend Lucie chatting with?" I asked.

"You don't know?" apparently my question was ridiculous because he looked incredulous.

"I don't own a TV; did I not tell you that?"

"Yes, I just forgot. He is a judge on "Road to Stardom" which is the country's top rating show and he's also a record producer. His name is Nathan Tanzey. Ring any bells?"

"None."

He gave a wide grin. It occurred to me that our whole relationship was based around ignorance. That was specifically my ignorance of all things TV-related.

We stopped and chatted to a nice group of people who worked on one of Teddy's shows worked on. They seemed all very friendly and confident. And they all looked extremely fit. I guess it was all that outdoor work.

Its not that I am unfit, in fact I run, but I don't actually look fit I wouldn't think.

And they were all lightly tanned just like Teddy. I did notice most of them seemed quite deferential to him. I wasn't sure if it was because he was the show's star, or because it was his party.

Then we sat down and started chatting to two guys who were apparently were old friends of his

"This is Allegra."

"Dog girl," said one shaggy haired guy.

"Excuse me?" Did he just call me a dog?

"You're the girl who ended up in Teddy's ute because you were running away from a dog."

"That would be me."

"Well nice to meet you. Your glass is empty. I'll top you up."

These seemed to be Teddy's real mates. There was a lot of banter. The girls seemed nice, though maybe more like accessories than integral, but perhaps my judgement was way off. I just wondered if they changed often and that was the reason they seemed more peripheral.

After about half an hour we continued on the tour and Teddy showed me his front room and it was very nice, though stark. No pictures of family members, or friends.

"Ok so this is my new office." It was a room off the front living area. Unlike the rest of the place it was an actual room and it did have a door, it wasn't just a space. Also it wasn't grey but rather all wooden bookshelves. It looked like an old-style den or library.

"Great room." I said, "Did you forget to tell your designer the room was here? He forgot to knock the walls out."

He nodded "I kind of thought you'd like this room more than the rest."

"Oh I like it all really. It is just very modern. This room is very cosy. Did your TV people help with the design?"

"Louisa did it."

I thought I'd go with ignorance as it had served me so well this far in our relationship.

"Who's Louisa?"

"I am." When I turned she was leaning on the doorframe behind me looking rather seductive and rather pissed off. "I am Teddy's girlfriend."

"Louisa and I used to live together," he corrected. "We're taking a break." That was a very TV response, even I knew that.

"Well *that* is up for further discussion."

Talk about your awkward moment, I hoped that any further discussion would not take place then and was scheduled for another time and place, preferably one where I was not present.

Teddy sipped his beer. I sipped my champagne. That was another glass down. Louisa glared at me.

"Well you have done a great job with this place. Are you a designer?"

She looked completely incredulous. As if I was insulting her on purpose or something, which I might have done, had I had the knowledge base.

"No. I am a Louisa Lane. I am magazine editor and I have my own lifestyle program on 9 and the women's channel."

"How exciting for you! Gee, you must be super busy. I'm sorry I didn't know. I don't watch TV or read magazines."

"How is that possible?"

Another guest, the curly headed dude who had gotten my drink earlier had wandered in…apparently he didn't know it was an awkward moment or didn't care.

"How is what possible?" the dude asked.

"That she doesn't read magazines or watch TV."

"Really?" said the dude. "Cool."

"It's not cool, Guy, you edit a magazine." Louisa obviously didn't approach such things with Guy's laissez fair attitude.

"Well I don't own a TV because I think they are anti-social," I said. "No offence." The no offence was directed to Teddy not Louisa.

"None taken" he said and sipped his beer again. He seemed to be enjoying his party even if I wasn't so much, anymore.

"And I don't read magazines because I own a bookshop and I read books instead, oh although I do read the newspaper so sometimes I read the Good Weekend or maybe at the doctor's office I read New Scientist. So I guess I do technically read magazines."

"New Scientist is not a magazine," spat Louisa.

"Louisa it is, you know." Guy the dude corrected.

"Yes but not a popular magazine."

"I think it's popular among scientists," I added. She didn't think that was helpful or witty it seemed.

"Right on, dude." Talking with Guy the dude was like being back on a commune.

She glared at me. She glared at Guy the dude. She glared at Teddy.

"I need another Cosmo," she announced and she turned and left.

"There are Cosmos? Cool!" Guy the dude asked and followed her.

I wondered what it was that had drawn Teddy and Louisa together in the first place. On the surface they seemed like an odd match. How had they met? And why were they taking a break.

Teddy stared at me over his beer.

"Teddy, I think you two have some unresolved relationship issues, I have to tell you."

"It's pretty resolved for me". He grinned and walked closer. And before I knew what was happening Teddy Green was kissing me rather urgently on the mouth. And I must say it was rather good.

Now, I endorse the concept of the 'party pash', as it was known when I was a teen, as much as the next person, but to be honest I am not usually the person being pashed.

In fact I would have to say "rusty" would have been a polite way of describing me. But the funny thing is it seemed like the most natural thing in the world.

Unfortunately Louisa decided to return to the office and caught us mid-pash. She was not happy.

"I can't believe you would embarrass me like this," she screamed at Teddy and then threw her drink, including the glass at us.

It was like scene from a bad movie because everything went slow and silent, although of course in reality the band was still going, and then thwack the glass hit me.

It hit me on the forehead just above the right eyebrow. And man did it hurt.

"Shit" was the unanimous response from Teddy, her and me.

I'm not sure what she was doing next, except saying, "Oh my God, I'm sorry. I'm so sorry." Over and over.

And then the room filled with people asking what had happened. I looked for Lucie but didn't see her in the fog of faces.

There were lots of "shit Louisas". And a few people saying "you've really lost it this time."

And I remember Teddy pressing something on my forehead and saying.

"Everyone calm down. She'll be fine. The show is over. Go enjoy the party."

Somewhere in there I heard him saying "Louisa, you just need to go now."

And then I saw some of my own blood, which I have never been good with, and then I passed out.

When I came around I was in the back of Teddy's car, which Jane was driving.

"She should charge Louisa with assault, Teddy" I could hear Jane saying "That would serve her right."

I blinked and his concerned face was hovering over me.

"Hey Allegra, how are you doing? We're taking you to casualty to get your head looked at, OK?"

"OK. I'm sorry I ruined your party Teddy."

"Baby you didn't ruin it". Now I was baby! "How can you even think this was your fault?"

"Well, I just think…"

"Don't think about it now, OK?"

"Is Louisa OK?"

"Don't you worry about her, I'll take care of her." said Jane.

"She's fine. How about you just focus on yourself," added Teddy.

"Oh"

"What's wrong?"

"I didn't get to finish the house tour."

"Another time. Look, we're here."

Casualty was pretty quiet but even so I think Teddy flirted with the nurses because I was in and attended to pretty quickly for person who presented with a fairly minor complaint on a Saturday night. We didn't talk much while we were waiting. I was just thinking how I really should have stayed home, and I am not too sure what he was thinking about, maybe gardening. And I was a bit worried about Lucie; I didn't like leaving her alone and at the mercy of Nathan the Lizard man.

The nurse was really nice and friendly and kept asking Teddy questions about other celebrities and what really went on behind the scenes at the Logie Awards.

By the time we were done and I'd had my stitches in and we got back to his place it was about 1am so I guess it took longer than I thought. The party had kind of died I guess and the band was packing up.

He laid me on the couch while he and Jane farewelled the stragglers.

"Well, I'd better be getting home then. Can you call me a cab, please?" Apparently Lucie had left with the Lizard, as I'd feared.

"Why don't you stay here?" Uhm I can think of several reasons. The one I gave was.

"I have to be home to open the shop tomorrow."

"Can't the owner do it?" Jane asked.

"I am the owner."

"Wow the rent must be dear over there."

"I suppose."

"Well Teddy can you take Allegra home then? Are you OK to drive?" He assured us both he was.

And so it was that at 2.30 on Sunday morning Teddy Green and I traipsed up the stairs to my apartment, neither of us feeling all that fabulous.

CHAPTER FOUR

The phone was ringing in my dream. And then it kept ringing and I realised it was ringing for real and not just in my head. And there I was waking up in my bed and there was Teddy lying there too. He rolled over and answered the phone.

"Allegra Johnson's phone. Who is speaking please?"

"Oh hi, I'm Teddy. Well she's sleeping right now…oh hang on she's waking up."

He turned to me and said nervously "Shit, Allegra, It's your mum."

"Don't worry Teddy" I whispered as he handed me the phone. "She will be beyond thrilled a man answered my phone." Why did I say that? Ouch, my head hurt when I sat up.

"Hi Mum."

"Good morning Allegra, I've asked you to call me Moonbeam, not Mum."

"OK hi Moonbeam." I rolled my eyes. I just couldn't get used to calling her that.

"And there is no need for the sarcasm."

She changed her name when I was about eighteen and we were no longer living together. After that long calling her Mum, it was hard to switch gears. Plus my younger sister's name is Stella Moon, which I am sure is no coincidence; in short it just confused the hell out of me.

"Sorry, I'll try to work on that."

"So who answered the phone?"

"Just a friend."

"Right, well why don't I know about him?" Ah, the reasons were to numerous to count.

"Well, maybe because it's none of your business, or maybe because you haven't returned my calls in over a month."

"I've been busy. I do have a life you know."

"Well mother, so do I." There was a long awkward pause. "So why are you calling at long last?" I wasn't looking at Teddy during this exchange because I figured I would have to explain it all to him after anyway. Most mothers are not called Moonbeam after all; they have nice normal names like Jane or Joy, Jeanette or Joanna.

"Well, I'll be perfectly honest with you…."It wasn't like my mother to be lost for words, unless she had an unreasonable request. I glanced at the clock and it was 9.45am.

"Please be honest. And maybe speed it up because I have a throbbing head-wound so I'm not much in the mood for chatting just now. Also, I have to go and open the shop."

"Of course you do, because you have a business and an income and plenty of money."

OK, note the money reference. That was my clue that she needed some money or more specifically, some of my money. Nice of her to care about my head wound, not at all, I thought.

"Cut to the chase how much do you need and why?"

She then began a tale rather light on the details that inferred her latest boyfriend had ripped her off and left her penniless. I know that I sound insensitive but this was quite a pattern of late. This was at least the second time this year. Different boyfriends of course but the same exact story. She really could pick them!

It seems being a free spirit was getting increasingly expensive for my mother, and in turn for me.

"I need quite a bit."

"Look Mum, it's Sunday and I have to go to the bank to help you and they are not open today. So why don't you call me back tonight after closing and I'll talk to you then."

"Allegra, I hope you won't let me down."

"Maybe it would do you good to know what that feels like." That was not nice I know. I don't normally talk back to my mother. It makes no difference except it makes me feel petty and mean-spirited. That was not a look I wanted to go with in front of Teddy. Maybe it was my sore head making me do it.

"Don't get all self-righteous, Allegra, I had to follow my own path, you know that."

"Well maybe today my path does not involve lending you money…sorry giving you money…but we'll see. I'm sure it will. Look, I have to go. Just call me tonight."

So there I was sitting on my bed in my PJ's with this damn hot guy, and a bandage on my head and I am sure he thought I sounded totally horrid, because he couldn't hear anything that my mother was saying anyway. It probably just sounded like I was being unjustifiably rude to my mother. And on top of that I knew squat about his mum but I was pretty sure he was the kind of guy who spoke to her nicely.

"Are you OK?"

"My head hurts." He handed me some Panadol and water.

"From the cut?"

"Yes, partly the cut and partly from that phone call."

"She sounds like an interesting character."

"That is a polite way of putting it. I love my mother, but there was an American girl who lived with us for a while and she used to say "Ally, your momma is a piece of work" and I think that is a fair description."

It was 9.55am. I started to hop up.

"Listen Teddy, I have to go run the shop today. Lucie only works every second week and it can be quite busy on a Sunday."

"You should be resting."

"Not today." I hopped up and twirled my hair into a flippy ponytail with one of my favourite antique clips.

I grabbed a t-shirt and knickers and a bra from the ancient drawers under my bedroom window. I made sure to choose matching knickers and bra so Teddy wouldn't think I was too skanky. Then I hurried off to the bathroom. I had a one-minute shower and pulled on my clothes. I washed and moisturised my face and flicked on some mascara and lip-gloss…basically I figured I wasn't going to look great whatever I did, so why waste the time.

Scenes from the previous night were swirling about in my brain. Fragments of moments. There was the kiss. It popped up a lot. There was Louisa's face. There was the glass flying through the air. A moment or two in casualty.

There was an image of Teddy making me a nice cup of tea at 3am while I popped on some snuggly but deeply un-romantic PJ's. There was the sound of his phone filling with text messages. And then there was the image of him tucking me into bed and lying down opposite me looking all-perfect in his worry.

And I remembered his exact words.

"Allegra, I am so sorry this happened. It was just bad timing" and then he had kissed me on the forehead and we'd gone to sleep.

I wondered what he made of my incredibly girly bedroom with its white lace bedspread, collection of antique hair clips and vintage clothes hung up. It was the antithesis of his new designer pad.

When I came out of the bathroom Teddy was leaning on the doorframe in last night's t-shirt and jeans and holding two cups of tea. Damn if he didn't look good!

"Well we'd better get to work." He said offering me a cup.

"We?"

"Allegra you shouldn't even be working at all! You can't run a business alone today."

He was heaven; well he was heaven apart from the psycho girlfriend. Maybe I could overlook that for a cup of tea and a helping hand.

"Well I am sure you have better things to do. Don't you celebrities "do lunch" or something?"

"Not today." And he looked kind of sad. I thought about bringing up Louisa, but I decided against it.

"OK then, let's go open up."

My bookshop is really very cute. It has a large plate glass window at the front, as shops do. And you enter through a door on the left hand-side of the window. There is a wide shelf along the window on top of which we display books. At that time I was doing a Jane Austin window namely because there was Jane Austen buzz because of some ABC programming. Listen you need to know that just because I don't watch TV doesn't mean I don't know what other people are watching. And additionally, what second hand bookshop wouldn't have many a Jane Austen novel they need to sell?

Resting against the shelf are two wing chairs with a small display table between them. Sometimes people like to sit and read or just sit and decide. Additionally there is the bonus that when it's dead quiet I then have somewhere comfy to sit. When my grandmother ran the shop she had a table with bargain books in that spot but the cosy chairs are a nice change.

Did I tell you my grandmother used to own this shop?

Really, I haven't changed much else since she died. I have a basket of children's toys under the display table so women can browse a bit. We don't really do children's books but I have a row of them because you don't want to discourage the kiddies from reading. I restrict that to classics, basically. Think Roald Dahl, think *Where the Wild Things Are*, think *The Hungry Caterpillar*, and various Children's Book Council winners. Well you have to have a system and I would rather encourage them to read good books than bad.

So if you look in the window you see the chairs and then rows of books shelves like in an old library. Recessed in behind the door on the left is the counter and cash register. That is my little nook.

Then you step down to a room with an old table and mismatched chairs around it. People think this is very designer and shabby chic, but in fact my grandmother found all the chairs at council clean-ups and garage sales. She was all about function, not fashion in the bookshop. Oddly in the rest of her life she was quite the fashionista.

I have added matching cushions because the chairs for the most part are very uncomfortable. The walls are lined with books in there too. That is where all the crime and romances are. They are back there because it seems these days that is really what most people want and it draws them right into the store that way. If I put Patricia Cornwell, Maeve Binchy and John Grisham at the front door many people wouldn't make it any further. After all commercial fiction is commercial because it sells and it sells because that is what most of us enjoy reading.

Around that table is where we hold book clubs. Sometimes a group of students wander in from the high school to research essays. These are usually kids I know or know of. It is a bit cooler to hang here than a library for the more alternative students. And frankly I quite like the company.

Behind that room is a bathroom, a kitchenette, an office and a storage room, full of books and books and more book. The office is pretty much the same as when Gran had it. I have a laptop so I haven't had to set-up a computer in there. It was her special place and she ran all her affairs from there so I don't want to change it. It's like her soul still hangs about in there or something.

My normal hours are 10am-6pm. On Sundays we go 10am-4pm but if it's busy I just hang around. If someone else is working they might call me down from upstairs. The thing with Manly is it's very hard to tell. It's a village style community but it's also a tourist destination so some days its extra busy and some days reasonably quiet. We are close enough to the Corso to get some of the action but not all of it.

So at 10.05am when Teddy and I opened the door old Mrs Carmody was already waiting. She was on her way back from church. She popped in most Sundays unless one of her kids was coming to take her to lunch.

"Hello darling. Oh dear what happened to your head? Oh I hope he didn't do that."

She cocked her thumb and looked accusingly at Teddy who stood behind me with the teacups while I unlocked and turned off the alarm.

"Heavens no Mrs Carmody. I just had a little accident."

"Well are you OK, dear?"

"I'm fine." She was still eyeing Teddy suspiciously, first out of protectiveness and secondly because I am sure she recognised him but couldn't place from where.

"So how was this week's batch?" I asked. She was working her way through every Agatha Christie ever written.

"Great. She really sucks you in that woman."

Mrs Carmody plopped down in one of the wing chairs while I opened the blinds and turned the lights on throughout.

"Just pop those on the counter dear. I can tell it's your first day here." She instructed Teddy in the shop etiquette, as if she herself were an employee.

I showed Teddy how the till worked, it is an old fashioned one so it's not hard. I also explained how to write up a receipt in the old-fashioned order book. So I basically answered requests and he manned the till.

He seemed to be really enjoying himself. He was chatting away to people, and having a grand time.

Some people recognised him "Hey aren't you Teddy Green?" or "Man what the hell are you doing here?" Good question buddy. What the hell was he doing here? He signed a few autographs and even posed for a couple of photos. He was very good-natured about it but I must say it did seem rather bizarre.

People who were regulars or knew me found it especially amusing.

And then there was a lull at about 11.30am.

"This is great fun Allegra. What a cool job."

"You think so?"

"Yeah, nice books, nice people, great location. What's not to love?"

"Exactly! I do love it, but you know it's not an adventurous career choice."

"How did you get into this?"

"My grandmother, Moonbeam's mother, owned the shop. When I came to live with her she set me up in the flat and when she died she left me the shop. So here I am."

"Wow. How did Moonbeam feel about that?"

"It was, shall we say, quite a scene. Mum, shouldn't have been surprised but she was. It's one of the many things she hasn't quite forgiven me for. Not that she would have done anything but sell the business anyway."

About then I realised that I was starving and feeling a little light-headed. So I left Teddy in the shop and ran in to the café to order some banana bread and some coffees from George.

When I came back Teddy was behind the counter and standing there talking to a customer.

For a moment he literally took my breath away, which is pathetic, I know.

I took a moment to just take it in. Here was one of the most fantastically handsome men I'd ever seen, and apparently many women around the nation agreed, and he was standing in my shop. Another interesting thing to observe was that he seemed to be exceedingly normal although it did occur to me that I really knew nothing at all about him.

He looked up and smiled at me. And he looked genuinely happy I had returned. It made me want to smile till my cheeks hurt.

Frankly it was all a bit much for me to get my tired and bandaged head around.

"You will be pleased to know I turned over $25 in your absence."

"Good, that will pay for the snacks then."

"Yes and then someone called Lisa called."

"OK", I imagined Lisa was now on the phone to Caroline screaming at her.

"Yes, she wanted me to remind you that she needs to know if you're bringing a date to her wedding." Boy was she subtle? "She was very particular to tell me that she thought it would be nicer if you did."

"Well I'll have to call her later. Did she ask why you were here, by chance?"

"No and I didn't tell." He gave me a cheeky wink.

Terrific. I was going to have a few phone calls to make tonight that was for sure.

"So when is the wedding? And who is Lisa to you?"

"The wedding is in three weeks and Lisa is one of my oldest friends. I'm a bridesmaid. And I am indeed wearing pink. It wouldn't be a wedding otherwise."

"I'd like to see that."

Was he joking? I figured he was.

"You should be so lucky." I tossed him his banana bread.

A family group came in and started browsing. The mother was a semi-regular so I promptly ignored Teddy and began exchanging pleasantries with her. I could see the kids looking at Teddy, trying to figure out what he was doing there. And so the day continued.

He got us a couple of pies about 1pm and more coffee. I figured he was normally a juice-bar kind of a guy but with a hangover from a lack of sleep, you need coffee and a pie.

There was peaceful calm while we scoffed our lunch.

"This place really has a great feel Allegra. It sneaks up on you."

"A little more mundane than making a TV show I guess."

"Well yes and no. There is certainly lots of hard work on the show. I do a ton of gardening and landscaping and there is lots prep work. There's a lot more to it than you see on TV."

"You mean more to it than I don't see on TV," I winked.

"Ah, yes." He chomped on the last of his pie. "I love the gardening and design. That's my first love and what I studied for, the TV stuff I just fell into."

"So, would you say you're a reluctant celebrity?"

"I don't know about reluctant", he said through a mouthful of pie. "Initially I loved it. Now, I don't know, maybe I'm tired. It is losing its buzz. I've been doing the show for five years, so it's getting kind of same old same old."

"So you're just in it for the money?"

"Well it has helped me build a nest-egg and the celebrity helps me to do things like write books and expand the landscape business I run. It just seems like the price of celebrity is getting too high."

"What do you mean? Hang on..." I helped a customer with the latest Wilbur Smith. The book had only been released that week but a regular customer had already devoured it and sold it on to me. "Sorry."

"Well just the constant recognition. The treadmill. The no privacy."

"Well if you don't like it, can't you just stop, return to standard landscaping?" Seemed easy enough to me.

"Sure, I can and I will but maybe I'm just not quite ready to let it go yet."

I was fading in the afternoon so bang on 4pm when the last customers left I pulled the blinds.

"Let me just balance the till to make sure that the "help" hasn't robbed me today," I said to Teddy as he sat down in one of the wing chairs.

He smiled.

"Do you bank the money Allegra or just carry it around in an unmarked handbag like your personal money?" He was still perplexed by my "cash in every bag" policy.

In truth, usually I banked it but sometimes I just rolled it over. Some days it didn't seem worth the walk to the bank and I figured I had as much chance being robbed on the walk to the bank as the shop did overnight.

Today had been a good day. We'd had a really steady turnover.

He just sat watching me and looking around the shop.

"How'd we do?"

"Great for a sunny Sunday." Sometimes sunny Sundays meant no sales, and sometimes great sales. I still couldn't pick it.

"How long did your grandma have this place?'

"She started it in the fifties before she had my mum. I don't think she expected to have kids so she set up this business instead. And then along came Mum or Moonbeam as she prefers to be called."

"Yeah, what's with that name?"

"My mum is a hippy, you might say. You can't say she's new age because she has been like this since the seventies so there is nothing new about it."

"What about your dad?"

"He's a reformed hippy. But he lives in Byron with his wife and they run a wholefood business. He comes down a bit though."

"Enough said."

"Mmmm. Mum lives in Katoomba."

I rang off the till. I didn't know how much to tell him.

"Well Mr Green, we'd better get you out of my life back to your real life."

Looking all sad he stood up and walked over. He leaned over the counter so he was looking me straight in the eyes. I was glad I had the counter to hold or I might have done a dramatic slide down to the floor.

"Allegra, I want you to understand this. I don't want to get out of your life, or for that matter go back to my life." And he kissed my forehead like last night. And then he kissed me gently and longingly on the lips until I thought me legs really would go from beneath me.

"Well, do you want to go home?"

"No, but I guess I have to."

"OK and I should get my van back. It's probably missing me."

"Allegra, I'll bet it is."

When we got to his street I could see the lights were on in his place.

"Will Louisa be there?" We hadn't really discussed her at all.

"I expect she will."

"Tell her I haven't decided yet whether I'm going to charge her with assault or not."

"Are you really going to do that?" He seemed surprised that I would even consider it.

"Of course not, but she doesn't know that." I smiled. He smiled back.

"If it makes you feel better, I'm sure she feels terrible."

"Well, it doesn't make me feel better. I'm a pacifist and whenever someone resorts to violence it just makes me feel a bit sadder about the world and where it's heading. How many wars have begun because of a kiss?"

"Well let's hope there is no war."

"Well just in case, I want you to know that even if you had invited me," which he hadn't, "I wouldn't come in."

He kissed me again as I got out of the car. It didn't help me want to leave and it didn't make me feel any better about Louisa being inside.

I wound down the window as I drove past him as he went up his front walk." Thanks for your help today."

"Oh baby, you're so welcome."

And there was that baby thing again.

Driving home I couldn't help but wonder how a week can change you life.

It was only this time last week when I was sitting in my flat just minding my own business when Teddy Green walked into my life.

He felt solid to me, but he also felt scary.

He had a lot of things going for him. He was a great kisser. He was damned cute. He had an interesting job. He seemed kind. He had a great home, although it was sterile and decorated by his ex-girlfriend who thought she was still his girlfriend.

And of course there were quite a few cons.

One was that he had a great home, although it was sterile and decorated by his ex-girlfriend who thought she was still his girlfriend.

Another was that we had nothing in common. Also there was the whole celebrity thing which was just kind of weird. And he knew nothing about my life or me and I knew even less about him.

Finally, I just wasn't quite sure I was ready to have my heart broken in such a public way. It's humiliating enough being dumped by someone who nobody even cares about but when it's a celebrity I expect it's much harder.

A little thing you need to know about me is that I am just not that great at the whole dating and relationship thing.

Don't get me wrong I am totally into guys and all of that, but I'm just not very good at it.

My friends think that I'm asexual, in that I give off absolutely no sexy vibes whatsoever, even when I am really into someone. And sadly that is not too often.

I've had a few boyfriends but none recently. It just hasn't felt right lately.

The first one or two of my boyfriends were in it purely for the sex. There is nothing wrong with that per se, and pretty much normal for guys of that age I think, but it was just not enough for me.

Growing up on a commune as I did, sex never had the mysterious quality it did for other kids. It was all out there on display. I have visited many "clothing optional" communities as well, what normal people call nudist colonies, so that pretty much meant that I saw the human body in all its forms from the get go.

The number of times I witnessed people in various states of arousal, foreplay and intercourse as a child are too numerous to count.

Other people in the throws are really not that attractive, for your information. They may think they are, but in truth, sex is just not that pretty.

The whole porn industry is, in fact, a total mystery to me, I guess those actors and actresses are at least, somewhat attractive before they get their gear off, which isn't always the case on a commune. Even so porn is lost on me.

I just think it is a private thing, I suppose.

More than anything else I guess I learnt early that sex was a guarantee of nothing.

Certainly, it does not guarantee monogamy, probably not commitment, not intimacy and sadly not even recognition in some cases.

In the end it just hasn't seemed overly worth the effort I suppose.

With my last boyfriend Connor, I went out on a limb and was head over heels and desperately in love with him. We were together about six months. He was smart, funny, cute and popular.

I found his love of cricket and rugby almost mysteriously alluring. He was your classic straight-up North Shore private school boy who worked in a bottle shop part-time and was studying Economics-Law. He was totally average in all the good suburban ways, I thought.

I think he found me, well, when I think about it I'm not precisely sure what attracted him to be with me. I think partly I was a change from the blonde bobs he usually dated. The girls exactly like my school friends. I think the fact that I ran the bookshop and was independent helped. Really, on reflection, it's hard to say what it was. I thought we were great together so I guess I didn't really think about what he thought.

Then I took him to meet my mother for the weekend. It was supposed to be a romantic mountain escape. You know the type. Fluffy jumpers, red wine, great sex, open fires and lots of taking our relationship to the next level.

Well there was sex and our relationship certainly changed but just not quite the way I planned.

My mother shared some of her marijuana stash with him when I went to bed early with a bad cold and promptly slept with him. It was a hardly a fun thing to walk in on when I came out of bed in the middle of the night in search of ibuprofen.

I suppose to be fair I should say they slept together.

Either way it ended the relationship, and for some reason I just haven't been too keen to get back into the dating scene since. Some things take a while to bounce back from, I suppose.

And even after the fact Connor was at a loss to explain his behaviour. It was as if he had been transfixed by my mother and all moral judgement had gone out the window.

So to find myself on the verge of a relationship with Teddy Green was somewhat scary to say the least. Just being on the verge of a relationship with anyone was scary.

After thinking about Teddy, and then my mother some, I decided I wouldn't call her back after all that night. She could wait another day. I knew there would be a message from on the phone at home, but she could wait.

CHAPTER FIVE

Monday

Monday morning I got up and took a run.

It seems weird that a hippy child with a dog phobia would love to run, but I do.

When we lived on the commune, before my mother took me from Dad, he got into a jogging phase and so he and I ran together. We'd run over hills or he'd take me to the beach and we'd run wild there, after all, we didn't have much else to do. He had no job and I didn't go to school.

I'm sure he was doing it to retain his youthful demeanour but for me it was, and is, about that rush you get when you have the wind in your face and it becomes trance-like and almost spiritual.

I love that you can run anywhere. You pull on your sneakers and go. City or country, it really doesn't matter where in the world you are. You run and you feel the same. The scenery may be different, people may look different but the experience is ultimately the same.

My grandmother, who was a deeply lapsed Catholic, said it was the same for her with Mass. On a Sunday morning anywhere in the world you can walk into a church and you know exactly what is going on, even if you can't understand a word.

When I was finally at school I started in cross-country and won the district and state cross-country. And I did marathons until a couple of years back. I still run them but now I'm not competitive anymore. I just kind of lost the urge.

In a good week I still run about three times a week. I usually run down the Corso and then turn left and run up to Queenscliff or right and around the Bower to Shelley Beach. I love that part when I run past Grandma and Pop's old building.

There are lots of runs I really enjoy and living near the beach there is lots to see and beautiful scenery, although truly when you get in the zone that becomes rather irrelevant. It's all about your rhythm and your timing and not at all about where you are.

Sometimes dogs do chase me and guess what, I run a whole lot faster on those days. I do avoid places set aside for dogs like Curl Curl Lagoon and Forty Baskets Beach; after all why look for trouble? And leash laws in Sydney and people's respect for them are improving albeit slowly.

I have to say though that some of my worst running experiences have involved unruly dogs. I sat for over an hour on the hood of a large Jeep recently while a highly strung Springer Spaniel barked incessantly at me. I was eventually rescued by a couple of pre-teens on their way to the bus stop.

Anyway, due to my sore head I just ran to Shelley Beach and back. I was a bit out of practice as I hadn't run much the past week. I was very happy there were no dog incidents that morning.

Lucie was in the shop bright and early ready for a major gossip. We both were, because I was dying to hear what was up with her and the Lizard.

Lucie works for me Mondays, Tuesdays and Saturdays and every second Sunday. My sister Debbie works with me Thursdays and busy Wednesdays, we just kind of play that by ear. Sometimes Lucie works an extra shift depending on Debbie's kids and her studies.

"So? Tell me everything!"

As there wasn't really much to tell I did tell her everything, except the kissing bits.

Her everything was that Nigel the Lizard had taken her out for a drink but she had discovered he had a few kinky sexual interests that weren't up her alley, so she left him in Potts Point chatting up the next bright young thing.

All day I waited for a call from Teddy, but there was none.

That night the girls and I were at the Manly Wharf Hotel having a drink. We were enjoying the view and watching the people returning from work off the Manly Ferry. They were a hot and miserable looking bunch, and most of them looked rather enviously at us as they wandered past.

My friends simply could not have waited one more minute to see me and get the gossip on my weekend with Teddy. As a result they hastily rearranged their busy lives to gather for a post-mortem of the weekend.

"So tell us about this Louisa then, Ally," asked Caroline.

"Well she is attractive, and rather sexy I guess. You know long legs, loads of confidence, the throaty laugh. I suppose she is alright underneath." I replied sipping my drink and averting my eyes.

"She is not! She threw a glass at you!"" Lisa said.

"I don't know her well, of course but she was perfectly pleasant," I said unconvincingly.

"Oh she's that bad!" laughed Caroline. For us 'perfectly pleasant' was code for, 'not very nice but one can't say exactly why for sure'. The world is filled with people like that in fact. Women, particularly, who never say anything unkind to you but look at you in such a way that you know they are not that happy to have you in their presence but there is not a darn thing they can do about it, well certainly nothing obvious, but then Louisa had clearly broken that rule.

Some of these girls get competitive, some outshine you, some out nice you, some just ignore you. Really each "perfectly pleasant" has their own strategy. It's handy to have a code to describe people in public places. You sound much less witchy than saying "that girl is a complete horror show!"

"So she has the voice?"

"Yes."

"Does she have the laugh?"

"Yes"

"Can she dance?"

"I would guess so. Hang on, I saw her. So that is a definite, she can dance!"

"And she can drink?"

"That I saw too. Another yes."

"Hmm, the full disaster" said Caroline disapprovingly.

There is a group of women who for some reason are just born sexy. Or maybe they just turn 14 and morph. They have gravely voices, great tans, and great bodies, whether they are curvy or planks is irrelevant, and they just seem so comfortable in their own skin. They can usually play pool and darts, they can always dance and they know more about rugby than most blokes. They are the sort of women who can pick a dress up off the bedroom floor and put it on and look sinewy, fabulous and totally uncrushed.

I have the deepest admiration for these women, because they are everything I'm not. Smart, sassy and sophisticated. Having said that, I prefer that they don't hang around my potential new boyfriend.

We all sipped our cocktails.

"Maybe he likes you because you're different, Ally," said Lisa kindly.

"Or he could just be hanging with you to piss her off," added Caroline a little too honestly.

"Caroline!" Lisa said whacking her.

"Well it is rather a mystery," she added.

"It is not a mystery, he likes her because she is smart and fun and pretty" said Lisa. Lisa is the kind one in our group. She never says a cross word about anyone.

I completely adore Caroline but sometimes her forthright attitude wore a bit thin. She was, however, right in this case. I was the antithesis of Louisa. I am not sexy or sophisticated or long legged or lithe.

I am a rather pale girl with long straight dark hair. I am the sort of girl who not only runs a bookshop, but also looks like she should run a bookshop. I am quite curvy I guess, but not in a comfortable-in-my-own-skin way. I'm more an awkward, cross your arms over your large chest kind of a girl.

My mother is one of the aforementioned girls with the gravely voices. It's rather odd because we actually look remarkably similar, except for that sexual confidence which she has in spades and which I'm sorely lacking.

She is thoroughly pleased that I lack it. It suits her just fine. It's another thing she has over me. She does like to draw attention to it.

"Allegra, why do you always mumble? Why can't you relax? I think you should go to a Tantric workshop. It would do you the world of good."

I think she would find that I would vanish even further into my cocoon at a Tantric Sex workshop. My Dad has a good friend who runs these workshops and I have heard more than enough about tantric sex over a vegetarian tagine to last me a lifetime.

The girls were still going.

"Well whatever the deal is, he has kissed you and stayed over, and he spent a day in the shop with you, so even a pessimist would have to say you are in with a good chance." Caroline is a pragmatist.

"So now we need a plan." said Lisa "What are *we* going to do next?"

"*We* are going to do nothing." I replied. "I totally think that is the best plan."

"See Allegra, that is why I am married and Lisa is engaged. *We* don't do nothing, *we* act."

"Well thank you, I feel better now!"

"Look all I am saying is that fortune favours the brave." That was Caroline's life motto. And she really took it to heart. She was always doing things that were brave or pushed her outside her comfort zone. She travelled alone, she bungee jumped, she interviewed for impossible jobs and then got them.

"I realise that, but I think that it will seem really forced and unnatural if I pursue it. I mean it doesn't even make sense to me."

"Look Ally, I know you are a ditsy free spirit, and I love that about you, but honestly you sell yourself way short with that approach. As Lisa says you have a ton of things going for you and you never promote them or yourself. You run a business, you're well educated, you have great friends, and you run marathons for goodness sake. Don't be focussing on the fact that you have a kooky family or your last boyfriend was a dog and all that stuff you can't control. Just focus on all the great stuff you can control."

"She's right," said Lisa.

"You know I am!"

"What harm would it do to call him and say "thank you for taking care of me and helping me out, I really appreciate it. I hope I can help you out sometime."

"None, I guess." I was not going to shut them up by arguing, and they were starting to make sense. Either that or my drink was kicking in.

And so it was that they forced me to grab my mobile phone and make the call. And of course I got his voicemail.

"Hey Teddy its Allegra. Uhhm. I just wanted to say thanks for your help yesterday…and uhhm, hopefully I can help you out sometime. OK, take care".

"He's not answering." Ah well.

***

I met Lisa and Caroline on my first day at FernHill School for Girls.

I arrived at my grandmothers' at the end of January just in time to start Year 11.

Of course it was total culture shock. I had essentially taught myself up to the time I entered FernHill. I did do a year of late Primary, but then we moved and my mum filled in all the paperwork to have me home-schooled. That just meant she bought me a few second hand school curricula and handed them to me. I did do half of year 9 at an alternative school but it was pretty kooky and honestly half the kids had such behavioural problems it was more a lesson in survival than anything else. It was a good thing I love reading or I would be totally ignorant.

So, fresh from a lifetime living in communes and being home and sporadically schooled. I found myself in a hat, blazer, ankle socks and a rather prim navy uniform standing at the gates of one of Sydney's more exclusive girls' schools.

My grandmother had no doubt pulled a lot of strings to get me in. She was an old girl, or an alumni as they say in America, as was my mother, though she suggested I play down any mention of the latter.

She was great friends with Sophie Bowles-Smith whom it transpired was the daughter of Hortense Bowles, our school founder. So I imagine the minute she heard I was coming she was on the phone to old Sophie wrangling me a place. Most people who attend FernHill have their name put down on the waiting list at birth. As my grandmother didn't know about my birth till well after the event she didn't have such an opportunity.

On my first day my grandmother dropped me off at 8.50am and sent me into the office alone to find out where I should go and what I should do. I was painfully shy and felt incredibly awkward in the stiff new uniform. All the girls were in groups or pairs smiling and laughing while their mothers, and even some fathers, hovered around.

I honestly felt like I was wandering through a book like Enid Blyton's classic English children's book *The Naughtiest Girl in School*. It was like being in another country. It was apparently a country where everyone was neat and blonde and entitled.

I made my way to the office and was told who my homeroom teacher was and where to go by Mrs Anderson the school receptionist. She didn't realise I was alone at first, and then it dawned on her.

"Where is your mum, sweetheart?"

"She's away. My grandmother dropped me off." I was suddenly even more nervous.

"Well Allegra, we'd better find someone to show you the way." And at that moment in walked three girls just my age who turned out to be Lisa and Caroline.

"Girls?"

"Yes Mrs Anderson," they trilled in unison.

"This is Allegra Johnson and she is new to Yr 11. Can you girls show her the way to Mrs Simpson's room please and make sure she knows where the toilets, canteen and lockers are?"

"Yes Mrs Anderson."

"Allegra, this is Caroline Dawson and Lisa Parker. They are both Yr 11 girls and they are in your homeroom. They will take care of you while you settle in and show you the way."

"Oh, thank you."

"And Allegra?"

"Yes Mrs Anderson."

"Welcome to FernHill. I know you will fit in just fine."

Mrs Anderson I came to know was an incredibly kind, yet formidable woman, who was a great judge of character.

"So Allegra, which school were you at last year?" Caroline asked as we traipsed back across the quadrangle.

"Well I was home-schooled, kind of" was my honest reply.

"Home-schooled. Wild! Where was your home?"

"Most recently just out of Townsville."

"And so why are you here now?"

"I've moved to Sydney to live with my grandparents and they've sent me here."

"Where do they live?" The big Sydney question!

"Manly."

"Well Lisa lives at Fairlight and I'm at Clifton Gardens." I really didn't know exactly where those places were. "We've both been here since Prep."

She said it as if they were a club that could not be broken into. I didn't expect to make friends at school so it really didn't bother me. I was used to a fairly solitary life.

Ever polite Lisa moved to change the subject "So what electives are you taking?"

"2 Unit Maths, 3 Unit Art, 3 Unit English, Modern History and Ancient History."

"Oh I'm doing Art. You will love Mr Turner, he's fantastic! Oh this is our homeroom. I'll introduce you to the teacher. She's not too bad."

If you have never been within the fragranced walls of an all girls private school in many ways you are very fortunate. There is a level of bitchiness and snobbery that I hadn't experienced anywhere before or since. Maybe it's all those hormones, maybe it's the general tone, maybe it's the air of dissatisfaction the girls inherit from their mothers, but there is a certain quality about them.

Having said that in many ways they are splendid and empowering places or that was my overwhelming experience. The girls don't dumb it down because there are no boys who need their egos built up. There are wonderful opportunities for creativity, especially in music and arts. Most of the girls are rather obedient, studious and well-disciplined.

The traditions impacted me more than most I think because I had previously lived entirely without them. I loved the bell ringing ceremonies at the start and end of each term, May Day poles, Easter hat parades, school councils and peer programs.

For some reason those girls I met on my first morning took me under their wing. They loved coming down to Manly and staying above the bookshop with me. They completely adored my grandmother and her rather odd ways.

I'm not sure what the attraction was maybe because I seemed quirky and unconventional. Maybe because they were kind, or maybe because they really liked me. Whatever the reason we are all still the best of friends.

I just hoped in this instance taking their advice and calling Teddy wasn't a big mistake.

Tuesday

On Tuesday I finally called my mother back. She was spitting chips by then. She would have refused to talk to me had she not needed my money. The thing about her is she happily ignores me whenever it suits but she is not at all happy for me to ignore her.

"Hey Mum."

"Allegra, it's about time you called back."

"Busy. So tell me again how much he took you for."

"I prefer not to think of it that way."

My mother worked in a holistic healing centre in Katoomba. She did massage there. I knew she earned reasonable money, but for whatever reason, she never had any.

"Well Allegra, I could use about $10,000."

"Shit mum." Usually it was one or two grand "I don't have that kind of money lying about. How did you get done so badly?"

"That is none of your business."

"Well, I'm not giving you $10,000 for no good reason."

"There is a good reason. I need it. And I'm your mother." Here we go. She was going with guilt.

"You are my mother true but usually only when it suits you."

"I always took care of you."

"No, you didn't."

"Well I did my best, Allegra."

"Mum you did the best by you. Not what was best for me." I hated these conversations they were pointless.

My mother and I had a chequered past. Among my litany of complaints were that she had kept me from my grandparents my whole life, ripped me from my father when I was nine, moved me around the country at whim, denied me an education, handed me back to my father after seven years and then just left me. As an adult I was annoyed she resented my good fortune, never called and slept with my boyfriends. I felt like I had more than reasonable grounds for dissatisfaction.

"Look Mum, I don't know what to tell you. Right now, today whether you are or were a good or bad mother doesn't matter. Today what matters is that you are asking me to give you $10,000 for no reason and I can't."

"You can Allegra, you have millions. You just refuse to help me. That money should have been mine."

"Oh Mum, here we go. That money was never going to be yours. You think I'm a rotten daughter but you were the worst daughter ever. You didn't contact your mother for 18 years, even to tell her you were OK. You didn't tell her you'd had a child. Your own father died and you didn't know for years."

"That's all history Allegra."

"And that is the history that led Gran to leave things to me. I know for a fact before I moved to Sydney she was leaving it all to the State Library."

"She would never have done that!"

"I saw the will, Mum. And your section is a codicil. I talked her into giving you an income."

"It isn't much of an income." Her income was twenty-five grand a year.

"Well Mum for someone who supposedly lives a simple lifestyle it should be. It is supposed to be as well as your salary not your only income."

"Don't tell me how to live my life!"

"Then don't call me and ask for help." I hung up. I was sick of going around in circles. That was the first time I'd ever hung up on my mother. She would be ropeable.

I knew where her next call would be. She'd call Johno.

I know this because she has no shame.

Tuesday night was a book club in the shop. I usually hung around for these but this time it was hard to concentrate because I kept thinking Teddy should have called.

I wasn't sure what the deal was but I was pretty sure he had gone back to Louisa; she was clearly a better match for him than I was.

Still, that aside, a phone call would not have killed the man. After all, he was the one who had asked me to the darn party and he was the one who had wanted to stay over and help in the shop.

There was however a phone call from my great friend Justin.

I met Justin when I was 11 and my mother and I moved to the Margaret River region in Western Australia. Justin's folks owned an organic winery and it was a kind of co-op. They lived in the main house and ran it, but basically you could live in one of the three other small houses for free, in exchange for work.

By the time we arrived though Justin's mum had died. So it was Justin, his dad and his older sister Melissa.

My mum worked in the wine shop part time and helped with some jobs around the vineyard.

It was great there. I went to the local school with Justin. Melissa was 15 and at the high school. She was going through a rebellious, smoking and drinking phase, but really she was the sweetest thing ever. It's hard to rebel against a hippy father so her efforts went largely unnoticed.

Justin and I were in the sixth grade and we had a male teacher called Mr Thomas. I had never been to any formal schooling before but Mr Thomas was very relaxed, and I realised later when I got to FernHill, he didn't really know the meaning of the word formal.

Justin and I used to catch the bus together and eat lunch together. Basically we were best friends. We would explore creeks and play with his dog, Jasper.

Justin was very big on choosing what clothes I wore each day and dressing me up like a doll. We would go to the op shop and buy clothes. It was very "Pretty in Pink".

Justin was also the first guy I ever kissed. Subsequently it came as no shock to me when Justin announced he was gay at 18. I had obviously turned him.

His dad would take us for rides on his ride on mower. Or take us to town and shout us movies. He was a really lovely man. He had wavy brown hair and honest to goodness the longest eyelashes I have ever seen on anyone.

We were there a few months before my mother began an affair with Justin's Dad. I don't know how long it went on exactly…but the week of my sixth grade graduation my mother decided she was getting claustrophobic and woke me in the middle of a Tuesday night to say the van was packed and we were leaving right then. I didn't even get to say good-bye to anyone.

I left Justin a note and then kept writing to him wherever I moved.

We have been pen pals and friends ever since.

He is now a part-time fashion stylist and part-time travel writer for the World Adventures guidebooks. When he lobs into Sydney he stays with me and I love it.

"Hey babe I'm in London. I will be there this weekend as planned. I hope that still suits. I have my key somewhere. I have a stash of fabbo antique, sorry "vintage" hairclips for you. Not as wonderful as you might have designed if you'd stuck with it, but enough of that. Must remember not to leave them in my carry on or they'll confiscate them because of all those sharp points. They might think I am a terrorist intent on taking over the plane with a diamante clip. Anyway, will be partying and meeting my editors till then. Love you. Justin".

Ah well Teddy Green might have no manners but at least the lovely Justin would cheer me up come the weekend.

Wednesday

Wednesday I had Debbie lined up to come into the shop. Basically with my niece Simone's birthday looming I knew she needed the extra cash so I pretended I needed extra help. And I loved hanging with Debbie as she has always been nice to me.

When I first came to Sydney my dad introduced me to my two older half-sisters and brother. Johno Jnr was indifferent, as was befitting for a 24-year-old male, Rebecca was a total cow and Debbie was as sweet as anything. She knew my dad had tried to find me for the previous seven years and so knew what a big deal it was that I was back.

The other two knew also but couldn't have cared less, I guess.

She used to have me over for dinner and meet me for coffee and things like that. My grandma loved her too. When she got married she even had me in the bridal party, which considering her mum and Rebecca were involved, was most magnanimous.

Now that she has the kids I love hanging with them and babysitting. It's the closest thing to a normal family that I know.

She arrived just after 10am looking like she'd run all the way from home.

"I got caught at the school gate by a couple of mums, honestly some people have nothing better to do than gossip. A couple even asked about you and Mr TV!"

"How would the mums at school know that?"

"One of them was on night duty at North Shore when you came in, and another saw him in the shop Sunday." Good lord, talk about your grapevine. "Both said he looked at you very adoringly and they agree he is better looking in real life than on TV."

"Well he may have looked adoringly at me on Sunday, but its Wednesday today and he hasn't called."

"Oh, well there must be a reason." Debbie is so nice she doesn't see the scumbag in anyone.

"Well Debbie, I for one would love to know what his reason is."

Dad called about 1pm.

"Hey Ally, how is it going?"

"Not too shabby."

"How is old age treating you Dad?"

"Not too bad. You know what they say you're only as good as the woman you feel and I have the luscious Rosie so I'm good." He was probably fondling her in some way as he spoke.

"Thanks Dad, I think that may be too much information for me."

"Ah kiddo, loosen up. Now rumour has reached Miss Stella that you are dating a TV hunk and she would like you to photograph yourself with him because her school mates do not believe it."

"Dad!"

"I'm just passing on the message."

"Tell my baby sister that if I ever see him again I'll see what I can do."

"Good enough." My Dad was not one to pry. "Now about your mother…"

"She called you didn't she. I mean I knew she would and I still can't believe it. She has gall."

"That she does." We both sighed. My mother had more than broken Johno's heart. He was happy with Rosie now but that had taken a long time. It would be hard for anyone else to believe she'd call him when I wouldn't do what she wanted, but it was not so hard for us.

"Dad she won't even tell me what she needs the money for. And it is ten grand, it's not small change."

"It looks like she went guarantor on a loan for the last deadbeat boyfriend. She could lose her house, Ally."

"Well why didn't she just tell me that?"

"Listen Ally, your mother is a walking question mark. She is the eternal 'why'." His words hung in the air while we each reflected on them.

"You don't have to give her the money if you don't want to and you don't have to like her either. It's your call, you're a grown up, but we all make mistakes."

"Johno, I don't have that kind of money lying about. Every time I give her something of Grandma's I feel as if I'm dishonouring her wishes. She really didn't want Mum to have that money."

"I know. Your grandmother would be furious." He had to concede that. My grandmother went to the grave furious with my mother.

"And then when does it end? This is increasingly common. It wouldn't even bother me if she at least faked being a decent or interested mother in between."

"Allegra, I can't tell you what to do…"

"Dad that is exactly what most fathers do."

"Not this father. I'm a man who has made too many mistakes. I will say this though kiddo, we all know that the fact you have the money to lend is no thanks to her, but nevertheless you do have it, and she is your mother…and frankly if she loses her home I would be worried about where she'd go. She might even want to live with you."

"That's blackmail!" I was horrified. Could that happen? Surely not. But I knew it could. She had no shame. She would move in and make my life eternal misery.

"Honey give her the money and tell her to bugger off. Tell her she was and still is rotten selfish, if you want as well…but if I were you I'd be the bigger person just one last time."

I hung up on Johno and called my mother and told her I'd have the money for her the following week.

"This time I want you to sign a loan document for me." I said.

"A loan?"

"Yep, you can pay me back $100 a month, no interest." Honestly it was as good as giving her the money but it made me feel she was vaguely accountable.

"And what if I don't?"

"I'll sue you."

"I can go to the bank if I want a loan."

"Then do it. Those are my terms."

"What happened to you Allegra? You have turned so hard. You have all of that old hag's money and now you act as cold as she did. No wonder people leave you."

"Maybe I am hard. I don't know." She always could get under my skin make me feel like her behaviour was because of me. "It doesn't matter now. If you want the money, come down and get it on Monday and sign the papers."

"Fine."

"And Mum?"

"Yes."

"I wouldn't be waving my finger about people being left. Didn't someone just leave you landing you in this mess?"

"See you Monday, Allegra." She spat my name at me. For a hippy she seriously needed to get her chakras aligned. And maybe get some Feng Shui done on her life too because she was deeply lacking both graciousness and serenity as far as I could see.

There was no call from Teddy on Wednesday.

Thursday

Thursday was a normal day except for the bridesmaid dress fitting for Lisa's wedding.

There is nothing normal about pink and strapless in my opinion. Don't get me wrong the dresses she chose were pretty and incredibly Lisa. But for those of us wearing them, who were in fact, not Lisa, they were not exactly perfect.

The dressmaker was in Mosman and I met the girls there. I was feeling rather flat and dejected. I was mad as hell now that Teddy hadn't called at least to see how my head was and I felt pathetic for having gotten my hopes up over him.

They had all raced in all from work and looked rather flustered. Caroline works in sales. She sells medical products or drugs. No definitely drugs. Lisa is a teacher at FernHill where we all went to school; they do love an "old girl" on staff. She teaches third grade just now.

Lisa's wedding was to be a lovely family affair that was bigger than Ben Hur. Lisa has three brothers and so this was her mum's only shot at organising a wedding.

It was being held in the FernHill chapel and then at the Cottage Point Inn, nestled in the Kuringai Chase National Park in Sydney's extreme north. It was a daytime wedding and they were hiring buses to get everyone in and out of the park, which was a great idea. Then everyone could really kick their heels up. It was one of those weddings where no detail was being left to chance.

Lisa was starting to get anxious with the wedding only weeks away.

When Lisa gets nervous she loses weight so hers was the incredible shrinking wedding dress.

"Oh my goodness, Lisa, its got to come in again!" lamented Mrs Vorska the dressmaker, who spoke with a lilting Russia accent replete with the lovely rolling 'r' sound and the word 'the' replaced with ze. "Darling, you simply must try harder to eat. We can't have you passing out as you walk down ze aisle."

"Or worse people might not be able to see you!" said Caroline. Caroline is the sort of girl who puts on weight when she is nervous so she really had trouble grasping this particular quandary and her dress seemed to be expanding at each fitting.

"Well I told you to leave me till the last minute, Mrs Vorska. I've got sales targets and client lunches all over the place this month. There is still potential for me to expand an entire dress size," she said while the dressmaker tut tutted through a mouth full of pins.

"Caroline Dawson, you listen to me young lady," Lisa's mother was launching in. "You WILL not be putting on an entire dress size this month and that's that. I don't care if I have to come to your home and remove every Tim Tam, chip and full-cream dairy product. There simply is no more fabric to be expanding. We had the fabric imported from Italy and there was just this roll. That's it."

"But Mrs…"

"Young lady! There is no but about it. Here is your diet for the next month. No carbs…and no alcohol."

"I draw the line there." Caroline did like a drink.

"Fine drink or eat, but don't do both. And go running with Allegra. You can burn off some stress that way instead." We all knew that was laughable but nobody dared laugh.

There was clearly no point arguing with Mrs Burton. She was in full mother of the bride mode. It wasn't her most appealing moment but in her own way she was just protecting Lisa and her 'wedding vision'.

"And you Allegra," she turned on me "Are you bringing a date to the wedding? Yes or no girl?"

"Well I don't know yet. Lisa said there was no rush to decide."

"Well Lisa was wrong." Ouch! "You've got a week to make your mind up."

Ok, now I was thoroughly depressed. At least Justin would still be in town and would be going. I would have someone to dance with if nothing else.

I didn't usually mind being single that much, but when you have had a taste of the other and missed it, well it seems harder to deal with.

Lisa squeezed my hand. She knew exactly what I was thinking.

Fortunately Lisa's mother had dinner plans and left us alone for the end of the fitting.

"Your mum is so full-on Lisa. Is she driving you mad?" Caroline asked.

"Not too much. She just wants everything nice I guess. She is getting a bit tense though."

"Do you think?" We all laughed.

"All ze mothers they are all ze same." said Mrs Vorska. "Me I have seen much worse. You don't vant to know."

No, we agreed, we did not.

Caroline bought the first round of drinks at the pub after and we toasted.

"To the bride!"

"To the bride!" Clink, clink, clink.

We talked again about the flowers. We discussed Lisa's dress in intimate detail. We lamented the fact that Mike's mother kept calling Lisa to discuss things she could easily have asked Mike. We talked about the seating plan and that led to Teddy.

"I still think there is a perfectly good reason he hasn't called Ally." Lisa really was so kind.

"Well I don't know what it is."

"That's a real bummer!" said Caro bluntly. "But the good news is you can at least say you have kissed Teddy Green which would be more than any other woman in the room."

"She's right. Look at all these women dating accountants and dentists and living dull, safe lives. What are they thinking?"

"Lisa, you're engaged to an accountant!"

"Yeah, but Mike's different." We all sipped politely. Mike was very much an accountant, even if he was a lovely one. There was nothing different about Mike.

"Why don't you call him again?"

"I am so not doing that. I wish I hadn't let you talk me into calling him in the first place."

"Maybe he just didn't get the message."

"Of course he did. And even if he didn't, well, he should have called."

We sipped again.

"Let's order and then we can finalise the hen's day plans."

Friday

By Friday I was fully resigned to never hearing from Teddy Green again.

I got up and went on a nice long run. It was good to be in my own life and my own zone.

I had been happy with my life a few weeks ago. I hadn't been looking for anything. Nothing was harmed.

And really what had I been thinking? We had these totally different lives. Mine was all about community and the people I knew. His life, I imagined, was all about celebrity and people who didn't know him. I would never have fitted.

I just needed to block out the fact that this incredibly kind guy had wandered into my life and wandered back out again. It was as if it never happened, as far as I was concerned.

That's what I told myself anyway.

Saturday

Saturday Lucie was in the shop and because I knew Debbie needed the extra money and I frankly couldn't be bothered to work, I had her come in and help Lucie. I decided to go and cruise some of my favourite shops.

I wouldn't say that I exactly have a personal style but I do like kind of old fashioned and eclectic things. Long skirts and boots. Fifties inspired dresses and unique pieces. I like things with a hint of glamour but not things that draw people's eye. So a cute sequin trimmed cardigan or a skirt with an interesting print or cut, but no bombshell dresses. And I don't shop vintage only, per se, but I often find that in those shops I find things that reflect who I am, or maybe who I wish I was.

The girls say I was boho before it was fashionable but I'm not sure about that. I think I just like a wide range of things. Some days I look quite dressy and glammy in a full skirt and kitten heels and then the next it's a kaftan and braids. Maybe it's the latent nonconformist in me. Maybe it's that I'm really stingy and through vintage clothing and op shops I can get more bang for my buck.

I had a lovely day wandering around some of my favourite shops and reading *The Sydney Morning Herald* in an inner-city café. A perfect, peaceful and thoroughly unromantic day.

And I probably only thought about Teddy a hundred times. Oh, I was so over him!

CHAPTER SIX

Unlike last week, this was a typical Saturday night in the life of Allegra Johnson. In the absence of a better plan I was in my shop in my Chinese silk pyjamas sorting through the stacks of books.

I had Norah Jones playing on the CD player, a bottle of red wine and a bowl of popcorn.

My shop still has the original faded old roman blind with the tassel so I could pull that down and have privacy from the street outside. On the footpath beyond the window the revellers were heading past to the bars, restaurants and pubs that line Manly beach and the Corso. I heard a large group of guys, who sounded like a bucks night, go past towards the wharf to catch a ferry.

I thought about our plans for Lisa's hen's night in two weeks and hoped they all came together. I really needed to start organising a few of the last minute details. I needed to chase up some late replies, but there was no point calling people on a Saturday night.

I sipped my wine and started to sort through the books that had been brought in that week. There was nothing rare or unusual in the mix but they were all the sorts of books that would turn over quickly and help pay Lucie's salary. There were Grishams and Courtenays as well as a few others I found abhorrent. And there was a pile of Tim Winton's a young mother had brought in earlier that day.

The books are displayed on the shelves alphabetically but also by genre. Crime.

Romance, Science Fiction and so on. These days the Crime section seems to turn over the fastest, which I consider a rather sad indictment on society.

After a while I came across a beautiful old copy of *Little Women*. What fond memories I have of Little Women. I loved the brave March women and their adventures. Of course I loved Jo the most and wanted to be just like her. How I cried when she cut off her hair. I could so clearly relate as I still looked like a shawn lamb myself back then.

Certainly it is beautifully written but I loved it because of the sisters and how much they loved each other. It is still one of my favourite books on sisterhood.

And of course hair has always been a defining thing for me.

As a child I was not allowed to have long hair. This is a fact that always amazes people. They all hold that image of the flower children with the long flowing locks and the braided hair entwined with flowers. Well that was my mother. That was exactly how she looked. She was beautiful, exotic and long locked. I thought she was the most beautiful thing ever and wanted to look just like her.

However I had hair that looked like I had been to a male barber at best and the abattoir at worst. It was one of the first rules I remember having imposed upon me by my mother. Allegra must have short hair.

The very first thing I did when my mother left me was grow my hair. And as soon as I got my hands on any money, I would use it to buy hair clips, hair bands with flowers or headbands, hair scarves or anything you could stick in your hair at all. We couldn't wear anything but navy blue to school, of course, but the rest of the time I wore them.

And so began my collection. And people now give them to me as gifts, or hand me downs or souvenirs from their travels, so my collection of hair paraphernalia stands at two-hundred.

I rummage through markets, I scour bargain bins, and I pilgrimage to Victoria Springs, vintage stores and the ground floor of David Jones. I love estate jewellery stores or auctions that carry such exotic and beaded treasures.

I love having long hair now and it's a symbol of who I am.

So no wonder I sobbed reading Little Women the first time and come to think of it every time since.

I popped Little Women on the shelf and poured myself another wine. I expect that Jo would have enjoyed the odd glass of wine if she had been born in a different time, though I would gladly have traded my glass for a stable family like hers, full of love and sisters.

I checked my watch. 9.30pm. Ah well maybe it was time to turn in with a good book myself.

People wonder how I can live without a TV especially as I live alone. I didn't always live without one but I have for the past five or six years. My girlfriends say it is a natural return to my hippy origins. They say that as a form of reverse psychology, in the vain hope that it will piss me off enough to go out and get one.

For me the thing about TV is that it is isolating. And it's all consuming. If I visit someone and watch a show with them then that is social I guess, though it would be a lot more social if they turned off the TV altogether and we just talked. Watching on my own I can't see how that is a good thing?

When I first moved in on my own I had a TV. I loved that thing. It was my VERY best friend. I mean that, I was barely functioning. My life revolved around the Bold and the Beautiful and Superman and Ally McBeal. I saw more of them than my real friends. I nearly failed school as a result.

So I just had to go cold turkey and get rid of it.

And now when I look at families where the only time they spend together is watching TV I just think it's sad. So now I do the book clubs at the shop, read, go to yoga, meet friends and see movies and I totally do not miss it.

So when I got upstairs I hopped into bed, with another wine and a book. "Why the hell not Allegra?" I thought.

The phone rang and it was Teddy.

"Uhmmm…hey Allegra." He had a good strong voice, I thought; even though I was mad with him.

"Hey yourself."

"I thought you'd be out."

"No."

"I'm so glad you're in. How are you?"

"Fine, thank you. How are you?"

"Great. Uhmm fine…I'm back from LA."

"You were in LA?"

"Didn't I tell you I was going?" he sounded genuinely surprised.

"No. You did not!"

"I guess I didn't get a chance."

"Yeah, Teddy, that whole day we were together last weekend and there was no time."

"Oh baby, don't be like that." Here he was with the 'oh baby' again!

"Like what?" I knew exactly what he meant, like all snippy. "I am just saying I think there was opportunity to say you were off to LA and maybe why."

"Oh man it was this huge deal. I might be going global."

"Excuse me?"

"Sorry I'm really pumped. My agent is trying to get me my own US cable show. It's a huge deal. I'll be like the Crocodile Hunter of the garden."

"Who is the Crocodile Hunter?"

"Ah Allegra," I could hear a mischief in his voice, "What are you doing right now?"

"Reading a book."

"Well I'm in a limousine and I will be picking you up in five minutes to take you dancing."

"Have you been drinking?"

"There is a bar in the car, but not really. Come out with me."

"Teddy, I don't think so…"

"Please…I want to celebrate…with you."

My head was not up for this, neither was my heart. Oh yes and I was still mad at him.

"Teddy, I haven't got anything to wear and I'm not really sure I'm up for…"

"Hear that knocking on your door? That is me…so let me in…please! Come on."

Shit! I really hate being cornered. But what can you do in a situation like that? You simple can't leave someone standing outside the door.

"Hang on."

I walked to the mirror. For someone who was reading a book in bed I looked fine. But by all other standards I looked pretty terrible. Still not much can be done in one minute.

I opened the door and there was Teddy with the largest bunch of roses I had ever seen.

There were about 50 of them. Hot pink! I could hardly see him in behind them. His head peeped out the side.

"Sorry I didn't call this week." As he offered me the flowers he offered a sweet apologetic smile that would have melted the heart of way tougher women than me.

"That's OK." I said lamely. "Come in. I think we might need a vase. They're really beautiful."

He followed me into the kitchen.

"So are you ready to go out?"

I raised my eyebrows at him as I looked back over my shoulder.

"Are you serious? Do I look ready to go out?"

"You look great." As I laid the flowers on the table he reached over and touched the small scar where the glass had hit last Saturday night. And pardon the cliché, but my heart did a little flutter. "I'm so glad that's healing well."

"Look Teddy, I'm really not sure I am up for a night out." I reached up and got my largest vase out of a cabinet.

"Not even dancing?"

"I'm not much of a dancer."

"Really? I thought all girls liked dancing!"

"Well I am not 'all girls'. I'm not really into the doof doof nightclub dancing in clubs."

"Fair enough. Well what about tapas? We could go and drink sangria and eat and talk. I could tell you about LA." His sparkly blue eyes were so pleading, how could I say no? "Well I did only have popcorn for dinner."

"Perfect. We can't have you starving to death now. You go get ready. I'll arrange these beauties."

I hopped in the shower because I hoped it would wake me up. I wasn't sure how I felt. I looked at Teddy and I knew I was gone but I was still not sure what this relationship, if I could even call it that, was all about and I was still pretty mad he hadn't called me all week. Also even though they were an incredible bunch of flowers I still felt that wasn't quite enough. And the Louisa issue still loomed large.

On the other hand, he was taking me out in a limousine and he was in my kitchen arranging roses so that had to mean something.

What to wear? What to wear?

I did have a cute red 1950's halter dress that would look good with a pair of strappy shoes and a handbag. It wasn't very me. It was very Audrey Hepburn. I'd been talked into it and of course never returned it or worn it. As a result it was in pristine condition and ready to wear. I left my hair down and just popped a clip in. I applied the usual foundation, mascara and some red lipstick. In honour of the occasion I even added blusher and eyeliner.

I stepped out of my bedroom feeling pretty good.

That was until I saw my mother standing in the kitchen talking to Teddy.

I could see she was standing that little bit too close to him, and she was touching the flowers, leaning in and flashing her cleavage I imagined, though from behind her it was hard to know for sure. That was classic Moonbeam behaviour.

His eyes found me over her head and she turned.

"Hey Mum."

"Moonbeam, darling, call me Moonbeam," she corrected.

"You're a couple of days early aren't you? I thought you were coming Monday."

"Well I got a lift from friends and thought I'd surprise you." She walked across the kitchen and poured herself a wine. "I just met Teddy."

"So I see." Should I ask her out with us? Should I cancel?

"Did either of you want a drink?" she inquired sipping her own, or should I say, sipping my wine, which she had already helped herself to.

"Well we're on our way out Moonbeam so we'll say no," replied Teddy and he placed his hand in the small of my back. "You look great as always, Allegra."

"Thanks." So Teddy had my mother's number.

It seemed as if I was dressed up and I did have somewhere to go after all.

"Well Mum, the spare room is made up because Justin is arriving tomorrow, to stay. There is bread in the bread machine and hummus in the fridge. I won't say help yourself, because I know you will. Oh and that is the last of the wine."

"Nice to meet you Moonbeam." Teddy was politely extricating himself.

"When will you be back?" I felt 15 or rather the way 15-year-olds in movies felt because my mother never worried where I was or who I was with when I was 15.

"We don't know," called Teddy over his shoulder as we headed down the stairs.

Outside the air was fresh and I felt so good blowing my mother off that I almost wanted to skip.

Then I saw the car. It was the biggest, ugliest, flashiest gas-guzzling limousine I'd ever seen in my life and it was totally fabulous.

"Oh my God! It's fantastic!"

We hopped in the back and he poured expensive French champagne into matching flutes.

"How did you ever end up as delightful as you are with Moonbeam as a mother?"

I didn't even want to know what she'd said or done.

"She's like a walking 'what not to do' manual. Can we not talk about her, please?" I realised I knew nothing about Teddy's family at all.

"Let's have a toast."

"To big success and spontaneity."

"To big success and spontaneity." We clinked our glasses and sipped. And he leaned in and gave me a long, luscious champagne infused kiss.

"I'm really glad you decided to come out."

I leaned back against the seat and his arm was over my shoulder. It was a wonderful, strange, safe feeling that I thought I could rather get used to. Then I breathed in and reminded myself I would be getting my heart broken big time if I didn't keep my head.

"I love that dress, baby." He was fiddling with the necktie in an affectionate way. And there was the baby thing again.

"Thanks. Not very LA?"

"It's universally fabulous I think." Hard to argue with that.

"So, Mr Big Shot, I must ask..." He looked at me. "Do they not have phones in LA?"

"Yeah sorry about that. I forgot your number. And I could have gotten it but whenever I had free time it was the wrong time. You know the whole day here and night there thing. Sorry."

"OK". I wasn't really OK with it but I didn't want to seem petty. "But just so you know I'm still mad at you! In future, if you make the quick phone call you can save a fortune on roses."

"Noted." He kissed me again. I was glad the screen between the driver and us was up. Its very hard playing hard to get when you are with the hottest guy you ever met in a limo and you have, let's face it, been single a while.

I broke free and sipped my champagne. We were cruising over the Spit Bridge.

"So tell me about LA? What were you doing there?"

And so he launched into an elaborate tale about meetings and deals and contracts, all of which I didn't exactly get but the gist of which was he could be getting his own gardening show on the US *Homeliving* cable channel in a matter of weeks.

"So does this mean you'll be moving to LA?"

"Yeah maybe. Well, I think so...it just depends..."

"How exciting for you." Yes, for him exciting. For me, not so much. The good thing was that at least this news told me that he and I were out to have fun and that was because he was leaving town in a short while.

"Well nothing is for sure yet but fingers crossed."

"Fingers crossed." My face must have betrayed me because he pulled me closer.

"Look, Allegra, let's just see how things go. See if it works out."

I wasn't sure if he was talking about the new show or us or if there was an 'us' even. And I certainly wasn't going to ask.

"Absolutely," I said and chinked my glass against his once again.

The Spanish section of Sydney was pumping as it frequently does. Some people call it the Spanish quarter but as it only takes up a couple of blocks, it's not really a quarter of anything in particular, so I consider that a bit of a misnomer. It was a hot summer night and people were out and about enjoying the warmth and a few ales.

It felt weird to step out of the quiet seclusion of the limousine into all that hubbub.

We walked down Liverpool Street to a cute little tapas bar. It was a two-storey place with exposed brick walls and chunky wooden tables. It wasn't groovy and designer but dark and cosy. We had a corner table.

We ordered sangria and about half the menu. Olives, baby potatoes, stuffed squid, chorizo sausage, some sort of sardine dish, some chicken marinated in yummy spices and prawns in a sizzling little pot.

"So, what does your family think about you moving to LA, and where are they anyway?"

"Well my folks are in Bathurst."

"Did you grow up there?"

"Yeah my Dad is a high school principal and my mum works in a doctor's office. She's kind of an office manager."

"And your brothers are they there?"

"My youngest brother is at uni there. The next one up is backpacking in Europe and the eldest is working as an engineer for a mining company in WA."

"And what do they think of you working in TV?"

"They think its fine. You know, as long as I'm happy. My brothers tease me of course, and think I'm a tosser, but that's normal. My youngest brother Andrew just likes coming and crashing with me when he comes to town."

"So now he can crash in LA."

"Hmmmm, maybe." He sipped his beer. "Are your parents happy with your career choice?'

"Well, my mother definitely isn't."

"So you two aren't close?" I couldn't tell if he was being sarcastic or not.

"Not really."

"What about your Dad?"

"Well, hmmm Johno, my Dad, thinks I should get out and use my other talents or that I should have pursued other things, but he's happy overall that I have found a safe place."

"Have you been in many unsafe places?" he looked very concerned.

"Growing up with my mother was an adventure, shall we say. And communes are not always super safe, especially if your mother forgets to look out for you."

"You grew up on a commune?" I had forgotten he didn't know and it reminded me that really we knew very little about each other at all.

"Several communes in fact, and some co-ops too."

"Was it wild?"

"Wild is a good word for it actually."

"Wow! You are a woman of mystery. How old were you when you left?"

"Sixteen."

"Did you miss it?"

"Not for one moment." Well maybe the odd moment here and there.

***

My childhood breaks neatly into two sections.

In the beginning I lived in the Northern Rivers of NSW around Lismore and Nimbin... There was my Mum, my Dad and I.

I didn't spend that much time with Mum. I was often with my Dad though. These days he would be described as my primary caregiver. I didn't know exactly where my mum was a lot of the time and it never much bothered me. I had friends and I had Dad. He taught me and a couple of other kids to read. He and a lady called Skye would informally school us with songs and books and simple maths. We would cook and count and measure. Dad got an old set of Encyclopaedia Britannica's at a second hand bookshop and any kid's books he could get his hands on whether they were story books or school books or dictionaries and we would read, or do simple science experiments. I read every page in the entire set of encyclopaedias before I was nine.

That was the idyllic phase, I guess.

Then Dad went to Sydney for a few days when I was nine and my mother decided it was time to move on. She packed me and my belongings up, and she hopped in the beat-up station wagon she owned and she and I drove off into the sunset.

And Dad was gone from my life.

She told me it was a vacation so I thought we were going back at first. After a while it dawned on me we weren't on vacation and we weren't going back. She told me Dad had never returned from Sydney for us so there was no point going back to the commune we'd been living on as long as I could remember. At the time it made no sense to me but I chose to believe her. What other choice can a nine-year- old make but to have faith in the one who is left?

We went to Rockhampton, then somewhere in Victoria and then WA for a year, where I met Justin. Then we were up near Broome for a while and then in the Daintree for quite sometime, staying in a few places and then back to Rockhampton.

When I was sixteen she returned me to a father I no longer knew and she left me.

***

"And what about your dad, wasn't he on the commune with you?"

"The short answer is no, but it wasn't his fault." I didn't want to get into all that, talk about a mood killer.

"OK." Beer sipping and hand patting. I liked the hand patting. "What talents does your dad think you should be using, particularly?"

"Sorry?"

"You said he thought you should be using your talents."

"Oh yeah, well I originally intended going to art school to study jewellery design but I changed path because well there is not a lot of stability in that. So instead I studied to be a nutritionist ...he thinks I should be using my skills in that area if not my design skills at least, but since I gave up running I've lost all interest in the whole nutrition and fitness industry and mainly I like the bookshop."

"You run? You ran."

"Marathons. My figure was against me actually. You need to be un-curvy. Boobs are a big hindrance." I must have been tipsy, as I don't usually make reference to my breasts when sober.

"I kind of like your curves."

"Thanks, I think. I am fairly ambivalent about them, to be honest, but for running they were not helpful."

"So Allegra, let me see if I have this straight; you are a curvy, former nutritionist and marathon runner with a dog phobia, design ambitions a second-hand book shop and no TV."

"Hey that makes me sound both strange and interesting."

"How about alluring?"

"It's hard to argue with alluring." Especially while drinking sangria.

Some girls came out and started flamenco dancing.

"I told you there'd be dancing" he winked at me.

"Hey as long as I'm not doing it, that's fine."

"Have you ever been to Spain?" He had to lean in really close so that we could still hear each other over the music. He smelt all spicy and lemony. Some lovely aftershave, no doubt. I hoped Louisa hadn't given it to him.

"As a matter of fact I have."

"Really?"

"Yes when I was young I did a Contiki tour and we went to Barcelona, Toledo and Madrid."

"I can't see you on an organised bus tour, baby," he shook his head.

"Well, it was a good way to get a taste of travel, but maybe not a great fit for me. And you know there are lots of stray dogs in Spain."

"Oh no!" He was laughing at me.

"Exactly! Poor Lisa began asking me to stay on the bus whenever it stopped, lest she should have to protect me or calm me down."

"I can imagine. But I'm sure you were very brave."

"Well I'm sure I was very embarrassing. It's amazing that poor girl is still my friend."

We stopped talking and watched the girls swirl their frilly skirts and twirl their fingers while we nibbled our tapas.

"Is this Lisa the one having the wedding?"

"Indeed she is."

"Have you got a date yet?"

"Still looking. You wouldn't believe how hard it is to find a nice reliable fellow who calls regularly in this town."

"So I've heard."

"Anyway I am not sure if I even want to take a date." The sangria and champagne were starting to kick in and I had this feeling I was leaning in too close, which I try not to do as a rule in low-cut dresses. I could feel Teddy's attention wandering away from my eyes.

"Why not?"

"How can I flirt mercilessly with all the single men if I take a date?"

"Hmmm, good point. And I'll bet you're an outrageous flirt."

"Well if you mean outrageously bad then that's true." I gulped down the last of my sangria as he drained his beer.

"Is it time to take you home now, Allegra?"

"I think it might be."

"Well, our chariot awaits. Will it be taking you to your home or mine?"

Good question. My body wanted to answer "your place" but my mind was saying "my place."

He paid the bill and we headed outside.

"Who's living at your home Teddy?" It was a fair question since Louisa was there last time I looked. We climbed into the limo.

"Just me." He kissed me long and hard.

"Really? Well even so, I'd better go to my place."

"Are you sure?" Again with the kissing.

"Well, not totally" And again. "But my mother is there, as you know, and my friend Justin is arriving on a morning plane from London and to say he detests Moonbeam is one of the world's greatest understatements so…" He kissed me into silence. And all the way home.

When we got back I really did want to get out but you know how it is when you have been having an outstanding make-out and so your legs are jelly. So this time the body and spirit were both unwilling.

"Are you sure you haven't changed your mind? You could ask me up."

"I could…but I'm not going to. Sorry. I told you Justin is coming."

"Should I be jealous of this Justin?"

"You can be if you like, but I must tell you it would be a waste of your energy."

"Gay?"

"Totally."

"Fair enough." More kissing and some touching too.

"Still I could just come up for a little while…" He kissed me again slowly and deeply and longingly. Miraculously I held my resolve.

"Try calling me this time. It might improve your chances."

"You're tough, baby." I climbed out of the limo and up my stairs.

My mother was still awake when I returned. I didn't want to get embroiled in a discussion with her about Teddy, or anything else for that matter.

"Hey Mum."

"Moonbeam!"

"Whatever. Did you find some dinner?"

"Yes. I'm surprised to see you back here tonight."

"Justin will be here bright and early in the morning."

"Oh yes, that dreadful boy."

"Look he's just protective of his family-no crime there. Anyway, he's my friend, so you'll just have to be nice. After all, I wasn't expecting you until Monday."

"Hmmm. So what's with the new boyfriend?"

"He's not a boyfriend really. To use your own terminology, we don't want to label it." She was big on that whole not labelling things because that defines them and thus destroys them and who wants to be in a box style of conversation.

"Well how would you describe it, Allegra?"

"I think I would say he's just a guy I know."

"He's that TV fellow, isn't he?"

"Apparently."

"Well what's he doing with you Allegra?"

Ah she has a way about her, my mother. "Nice Mum, really nice. I'm off to bed."

"I'm simply saying that he could have anyone."

"OK, whatever."

"No need to be sensitive Allegra."

"Look, Mum, I'm tired, and I need some sleep. I'll see you tomorrow."

Nothing like my mother to take the shine off a night.

Despite of my misgivings, I climbed into bed and had very sweet dreams where I was being kissed by this extremely cute guy, who bore a striking resemblance to Teddy Green.

We were in a little house with a white picket fence and it had an excellent garden.

CHAPTER SEVEN

I woke to Justin pounding on the door at 7.30am. He had apparently mislaid his key.

"Hey beautiful one!" I looked many things but beautiful was not one of them when I opened that front door. "Justin has arrived."

"I can see that Juz."

"Now don't be all grumpy and bed-heady, Ally. Help me get all these bags in."

"What have you bought, you shopping maniac?" I have moved house with fewer bags than Justin takes on a trip.

"Oh you know just a few little treats and treasures, my pretty. Shall we put these in my room?"

"Bad news, my mother is asleep in there."

" EEEEEEEEEWWWW, that witch! Why is she here? I can't even believe you let her in. You seriously have to stop letting her manipulate you." He looked very much put out.

"I didn't invite her. She just turned up and I was on my way out on a date so I…"

"Excuse me. Stop. A date. Miss Allegra Johnson, you have been holding out on me. We have so much to talk about. Put that kettle on!"

By 10am when, I had to open the shop, Justin was up to speed on my 'date' and safely snuggled down in my bed after a big brekkie. I promised to wake him at 1pm for lunch and so he could get outside and hopefully normalise his sleep schedule a little, not that Justin ever has much of a normal sleep schedule jet lag or no jet lag, truth be told.

My mother was still sound asleep and with a bit of luck their paths wouldn't cross. Their mutual loathing knew no bounds and frankly I was not in the mood to be in the middle. All that sangria had left me with a slow throbbing headache and talking with my mother had left me with plenty of self-doubt.

My goal was just to get through the day.

I felt Sunday night was going to be the night from hell. Just me, my mother, Justin – alone together.

I was hoping for a miracle that someone would come and save me from the awful evening ahead.

The miracle came in the form of Teddy standing on my doorstep again about half past five. Did the man not own a phone, I wondered? How did he do business if he was all spontaneity and turning up whenever?

Anyway, there he was on the doorstep with a bottle of red wine and a bag of treats.

He leaned in and kissed me and whispered in my ear "I've come to rescue you." Had he been reading my mind?

"Rescue me?"

"I remember you said Justin and Moonbeam didn't get along."

"Quite right." He had been listening. He was too good to be true.

"Plus I wanted to see you again before I go out of town tomorrow."

"Oh, where to this time? Paris? Rome? New York?" We were walking through to the kitchen. The large vase of beautiful flowers he had brought and arranged the night before were on my living room table.

"Nice flowers," he said. "We're filming in Adelaide this week. We'll shoot two garden makeovers. It should be hot as hell but hopefully it will make good TV. One garden belongs to a foster mum who has had a gazillion kids in the past 20 years and the other family has an autistic child so we are doing a sensory garden."

It seemed to me that life had to get pretty grim before the powers-that-be in television land would descend and give you a garden makeover these days.

"Oh how terrible for them."

Justin came paddling into the kitchen.

"Justin meet Teddy and Teddy meet Justin." They shook hands in as manly a manner as Justin could manage.

"Oh you brought wine and cheese. I like you already." Justin said pulling things out of the bag and arranging the cheese and crackers on a plate.

"Well that was easy." Teddy had obviously thought Justin would be tougher.

"Buddy, I'm not your problem. Moonbeam will eat *you* for breakfast." The last part was whispered as we heard the key turn in the front door and Moonbeam sauntered in. "Not that she should even be here if Miss Ally wasn't such a wimp where Moonbeam was concerned. If you two date for a while can you help here get a back-bone in that department?"

"Not sure about that. How about I open the wine, though?" He said as I lifted down the antique glasses that had been my grandmother's.

"Allegra?"

"In the kitchen." Justin was chatting about his jet lag and how no matter what he did he thought it was worse coming back. Teddy was explaining how he'd come from LA the day before but his hadn't been too bad this time. I didn't like to suggest that might well be the difference between travelling economy and first class.

My mother walked in and stopped. She eyed Justin and Teddy chatting amiably.

"You two know each other?" For a woman who never calls, she can get miffed when left out of the loop.

"We go way back," said Justin. He was just playing with her head. "I dated a wardrobe fellow from the TV station for a while." No one knew if that was true or not and we didn't ask.

"We're having a wine? Can I pour you one, Moonbeam?" Teddy offered.

"Oh. Thanks." She was all charm and manners. I suspected she was already well on the way wine-wise.

"Allegra I ran into that sister of yours down the street at the shops, that Rebecca." Oh my goodness. Justin and I both froze on the spot. Their mutual loathing was legendary so it must have been quite a meeting. The only blessing was I hadn't had to witness it. "She has sure put on weight. I mean she never was attractive but these days she is beyond large."

"Did you speak to her?"

"Well, she asked me what I was doing here and I told her that I was visiting with you."

Boy if I hadn't needed a wine before I would now.

The only person who held more ill will towards Moonbeam than Justin was Rebecca. I suppose when your babysitter runs off with your dad to a commune it's hard to get over. And I imagine you don't want to run into the babysitter twenty-some years later while buying the newspaper. I would no doubt be hearing from Rebecca about this. Rebecca wasn't a bad person she was just a person whom life hadn't exactly dealt with kindly.

She had been her mother's sounding board when Johno left and any time she spoke to me or even Johno she felt like she was being disloyal to her mother. Her mother held on tight and wasn't going to let go. The curse of many an oldest child of divorce.

Plus she wasn't overly blessed with a forgiveness gene. Looking at my own mother sitting on the couch I decided Juz was right and I was overly blessed in that department. Perhaps a happy medium was optimum.

"Now, Teddy, sit next to me and tell me all about your TV show. I watch regularly you know, unlike Allegra." She was patting the sofa in a come-hither way.

He handed me my wine and pecked my cheek before he sat beside her and they chatted away about his job and gardening in general.

"I've done a bit of gardening myself, you know." Go Moonbeam.

Justin rolled his eyes at me and helped himself to cheese and biscuits. "Ally is a great gardener, Teddy. She built a vegetable garden on that commune in Rockhampton."

"I think it was a team effort," offered Moonbeam.

"Really? I remember the dude up there being mighty impressed a 14-year-old could single-handedly build and maintain an organic veggie garden."

"You did that baby?"

"I was hungry and bored so it seemed like a good solution to a problem." I replied.

"Wow, how cool."

"Hmmm…" My mother added through pursed lips.

You can't spend sixteen years as a junior hippy without being influenced a little by the experience.

Clearly the beat-up VW Kombi van is a hangover from my hippy days. My dad gave it to me for my 18th birthday. He had bought it to head north with my mother before I was born and he'd had it ever since. I needed a car and I guess he didn't need it anymore so it was mine. We lived in that van from time to time in the first eight years of my life so I have quite an attachment to it; it was in a sense my first home.

I'm not particularly materialistic which I think is another hangover from those early days. I mean I have certain possessions I love and I hoard books and love a hair accessory or two. But I am not into the acquisition of wealth for its own sake. My friends argue that is partly because through no effort of my own I am really quite wealthy, but they do also admit no one would ever know through my behaviour or spending habits. And of course I never tell anyone. It's about my only secret.

Another hangover from my commune days is that I can build stuff, fix stuff, and do without stuff. I could win Survivor if it really were a skill-based competition and not a mind game. Even better I'd thrive in one of those 18th century re-creation reality series. Growing up I had to draw my own water, grow my own veggies and bake my own bread. My mother was one of the less useful members of most of the communities we lived in but I inherited quite a lot of Johno's practical skills and resourcefulness. This was good in that it gave me something to do all day, especially in the wilderness years of my teens when my mother moved us around and Johno was out of the picture. It was also good for my mother who made sure I did her chores as well as my own, thinking no one would notice. Of course she tells the tale differently, but if we were left alone on an island she'd freeze or starve to death and I'd build a village.

Because the majority of these skills are not called for in day-to-day life, especially when you live a fairly urban existence, it always surprises people that the sweet ditzy girl from the bookshop has so many life skills. Bookshop girls are generally considered inept and bumbling and vaguely impoverished.

"Yeah, Ally, is remarkably capable you know", Justin offered. "She just looks all helpless and ditsy."

"Excuse me!"

"There's a lot I need to learn about you then huh?" Teddy said to me.

"Yes and we don't know too much about you either. So spill it. I need to know every last thing about you if you expect to date Ally."

"Justin!" I was horrified.

"What are you, her father?" Teddy didn't seem thrown.

"I'm her fairy godfather. Don't make me go get my sequined wand," laughed Justin. "So spill it. How did you end up with your head on TV?"

Justin was good. I'd never thought to ask.

"I was dating a girl who worked on a magazine." Ah Louisa was rearing her neatly coiffed head again. "She needed a guy for shoot, you know a guy who worked outdoors, so they could make him over all neatly…and so they used me. I already had a fledgling landscape design business, but I guess I wore the wrong clothes, which is good if they want to make you over. And then it led to a tie-in segment on a TV show. Do you know "Happy Homes" that used to be on?" Justin and Moonbeam nodded. "They got a ton of fan mail after my segment and it snowballed from there."

"So, basically, because you had the right girlfriend and looked hot you got a TV career?" That Justin, he cuts right to the chase.

"Uhhm, well I haven't really thought of it in those terms but…" Teddy looked awkward. Not sure if it was about the hotness or the girlfriend.

"Well lucky old you, I say. So what happened to the girlfriend?"

"We broke up."

"Like, back in the day?"

"Uhmmm well no…just recently." Teddy and I sipped our wine nervously.

"The glass thrower! Intense!"

And on that note Justin decided to turn in early, due to jetlag, which was a blessing I thought. Fewer questions and less Justin and Moonbeam animosity.

My mother however was going nowhere. And worse than that she kept leering at Teddy, which simply made me uncomfortable.

I really didn't know what was going on with Teddy and me but I surely didn't want anything going on between Teddy and Moonbeam.

"Teddy, do you want to help me get some dinner together?"

"No Allegra, he can stay and keep me company." She was good.

"How about we both help Ally out." What a guy.

So we piled into my small kitchen with her standing a bit too close to Teddy for my liking.

"So what are we having?"

"Potato gnocchi with tomato sauce and a salad."

"Cool, what can I do?'

I had already cooked the potatoes so I put Teddy to work mashing them. And I pulled down a jar of sauce I had made from organic tomatoes earlier in the summer and put it on to simmer.

Teddy looked at me quizzically "You jar your own sauce?"

"Uhmm yes." I was always kind of embarrassed by my love of cooking. It makes me seem like a possessed potential housewife or something. I mean you know you don't go to a club and discuss organic cooking; it doesn't get the men flocking. Ultimately though I just like to cook and eat well.

"Well, Allegra, that being the case I may have to marry you." He winked just so I'd know he wasn't serious. "I'll grow the veggies and you can make the sauce."

I noticed Moonbeams dark eyes got a tad darker and flashed a bit wilder.

"I don't know that there is room for a veggie patch in my flat or your designer terrace either for that matter," I laughed.

"Well, we'll just have to move to the country."

"Sorry can't leave the shop."

"I'm heartbroken," he feigned distress as he mashed. "I offer to give up my lucrative TV career and to grow veggies and marry you and you won't leave the bookshop!"

"Well, this is my home. I'm rather attached to it."

"Home is where the heart is. You'd be with me." He did have a point.

"Too many dogs in the country anyway."

"Ah yes, that would be a huge problem." He stopped and topped up his wine as well as Moonbeam's. While I briefly indulged in the fantasy of living in the country with him.

I folded the egg and flour into the gnocchi and rolled it out. I chopped it into little pellets and made small indents on the back of them with a fork before tossing them in the boiling salted water I had going on the stove.

He grated the Parmesan cheese while I served up.

Mum chipped in by setting the table. It was, by her standards, a huge effort.

We sat down to eat and it didn't taste half bad.

"Baby, this is the best gnocchi I've ever had in my life." Gotta love that Teddy. I tried to bask in his appreciation and ignore the look in my mother's eyes.

I walked Teddy downstairs. We decided to take a walk down to the beach. It was a beautiful night and it was so nice strolling along holding hands. Neither of us said anything for a while. It was lovely just being with him.

We reached the end of the Corso and hit the sand. Then we turned right towards Shelley Beach. We kicked off our shoes and strolled with the sand beneath our feet. The stars shone brightly, the moon was not quite full. It was magic.

I didn't want to be the one to ruin it by saying something goofy.

He pulled me very close and gave me the biggest hug I think I had ever received and I could feel his whole body through his shirt. It was a wonderful, warm feeling.

"Listen…"Shit here we go.

"Teddy, how about you don't start whatever you are going to say with listen, it just never bodes well in my experience."

"How should I start?"

"Well it would depend a little on what you plan to follow with but you can't go wrong with "magical, magnificent Allegra…"

"OK magical, magnificent Allegra, I am completely into you. But…"

I knew there would be a 'but'. There is always a 'but', you know. I wasn't sure if I wanted to hear the 'but'. It could be a 'but' about Louisa. It could be a 'but' about LA and bad timing. Or maybe worst of all it was going to be a 'but about me. Whichever way you look at it, 'buts' are never a good thing.

"Teddy, can we just not do this?'

"Do what?"

"Do the dump thing. I mean I don't even know if we're together and already I'm being dumped. Couldn't we just skip over it somehow?"

He looked at me kind of incredulously, as if what I was saying made no sense. I don't know why not.

"Allegra, I'm not dumping you."

"Well I just figured with the 'but' and all…"

"Baby, you are deeply paranoid!" He looked kind of perplexed. "Why would I dump you? Didn't I just say I was into you?"

"Yeah but you said 'but'…" Ok now I felt somewhat silly.

"Well what I was going to say was, that obviously because of the LA thing it's kind of complicated BUT I feel like we might have something here and that we should spend as much time as possible together before I go, if I go, so that we can work out what it is we have and what we want to do about it."

"Really?" I was stunned.

"Really. Well, that is, if you want to."

I decided a good way to respond was to squeal, jump at him, wrap my legs around his waist and kiss him. I think, as he fell down on the sand with me laughing on top of him, that he gathered my answer was yes.

There is something incredibly invigorating and exciting and yes, romantic, about rolling around on the sand kissing on the beach, in the moonlight. You wouldn't want to 'do it' there because as we all know sand gets everywhere but its great for kissing and getting swept up in the romance.

What I remember is feeling incredibly excited and right. Of course I also felt incredibly turned on as well.

So before he left, reluctantly, because after all a girl doesn't want to get herself in too deep too fast, he decided that the following Saturday when he got back to town, he would take me on the date to end all dates.

"Let's get this thing officially started right, Allegra." Which sounded pretty good to me.

So it looked like I was dating Teddy Green the very gorgeous garden guru. Now all I needed to do was not stuff it up, oh yeah and convince him to give up his exciting new international TV career to stay with me here in Sydney. Oh and I had to do it and in a mere three weeks.

Should be no problem, I thought, especially for a confident together girl like me.

Well it would have been no problem if I had been confident and together and there weren't other truly confident girls waiting in the wings.

CHAPTER EIGHT

Monday did not begin as buoyantly as Sunday ended.

That day I had to take my mother to the lawyer's office and get her to sign the loan papers.

How we had managed to avoid all discussions of the loan was really a mystery, but we had.

Over toast with Justin on Monday morning things were rather tense.

"So what time is your lawyer expecting us Allegra?"

"10.30am. I'll just open up and check in with Lucie and we will be ready to go."

"Fine."

Justin rolled his eyes.

"Don't pull that face at me Freddy-freeloader" she spat at him.

"I'm the freeloader? Excuse me, oh human sponge, I don't think so."

"Listen you two, cool it." I aimed at levity. "You are both freeloaders, OK?"

"I resent that!" huffed Moonbeam.

"Can't handle the truth, lady?"

"I am not a freeloader. I believe that the universe will provide. I believe in the natural order of the universe…"

"You Moonbeam believe in anything that will get you out of an honest day's work. Well, you will do some things for a buck the rest of us wouldn't. But what you really believe is that it is everyone else's job to provide for you, you old windbag.

Just be quiet and let us eat." Justin had crossed a line. You can call Moonbeam a freeloader, a sponge, even imply she is a bit of a whore but do not call her OLD that is the ultimate insult to her.

"Are you really going to let that ungrateful fag talk to me like that?"

I agreed with him, and I admired his courage but she was still my mother. That is the thing with her and I; ultimately she is always going to be my mother, for better or worse.

"No, I'm not. Look Justin, that's enough. And you too Mum, just stop it! I'm sorry you hate each other and it wasn't my idea to have you both sitting here this morning, OK?" Justin looked hurt and she looked vindicated. If she had been four years old she would have stuck her tongue out at him. "I want a nice peaceful harmonious life, like most reformed hippies do. So shut up and don't say another word, either of you."

"But…"they said it in unison.

"But nothing. That's it. Mum go pack, you can go home from the lawyers. Justin sit there and read the paper and eat your toast."

OK so the day was not starting well, surely it could only get better.

Where, oh where was the glowing, dreamy feeling I'd gone to bed with?

The lawyer, Dave McCallum, who had run up the loan form for me was the same one who had handled my grandmother's will. I still used him for all my legal business but he always came to me these days. I hadn't had the courage to go to his office since the reading of my grandmother's will. And yet, today I was going back with my mother.

I still didn't feel happy about lending her money. I knew my grandmother would be turning in her grave, but I didn't know how to avoid it.

I remembered all too clearly the day we had gathered for the reading of my grandmother's will and I have to say it was not a happy memory.

***

I Nancy Hawkins being of sound mind attest that this is my last will and testament.

I am survived by my daughter Sophia, also known as Moonbeam and my grand-daughter Allegra Johnson.

To my best friend Mabel Banister I leave my collection of 1940's records and my Jaguar, and my unit in Darley Street, where she currently resides.

To my long-time friend and employee Christine Wilson I leave $50,000. (I hope you go on the QE2 as you have always dreamed.)

For my estranged daughter Sophia, I have established a trust that will provide an income of $20,000 annually for the rest of her life. (I trust this will be enough to keep you above the poverty line but not enough that you blow the lot doing something crazy all at once.)

To my darling, Allegra, I leave everything else including the building housing the bookshop Read it Again, the business and the flat above. The building on Manly Esplanade housing the 8 units. (If possible I'd ask that you let old Ernie stay in his flat until his family moves him to a nursing home). I also leave Allegra all my jewellery, antiques and all my love.

Signed Nancy Hawkins 12 August 2000

That was how my grandmothers will was read. We were all sitting in Dave McCallum's law office at the corner of Darley Street overlooking the wharf. It was a week after my grandmother's death and I was still foggy with sadness.

Boats bobbed on the water, ferries came and went.

After the reading we stood. I turned to my mother to speak but she turned away.

Then I suppose she had a change of heart because she turned back and slapped me hard across the face.

That day marked a real shift in our relationship. I guess she had always had an issue with me or resented me for her own reasons. And she had certainly used me as a pawn when dealing with my father and grandmother that much I knew.

But that was the day she first saw me as more than a threat I think. And that was the day she decided that I was fair game. I felt from that day that she was almost out to get me. Call me paranoid if you will. And since then, despite my feeble efforts to restore our relationship, she has always come out fighting.

There are tons of examples but the sleeping with my previous boyfriend example is a real crystalliser.

She said she was just seeing how committed to me he was, but we both knew it was about taking something that mattered to me.

My friends cannot believe I still speak to her and I often think they are right but then I have a change of heart and I think, well, she is my mother.

***

Anyway that morning she reluctantly and silently signed the papers at the lawyer's office and then we hit the bank. I transferred ten thousand dollars to her account and really didn't feel any better about it.

It wasn't going to fix our relationship and I knew she resented me for having the money to give her in the first place so not really a great circumstance under which to loan someone money.

"Do you want to get a coffee before you head off?" I asked.

"No thanks. I'm heading back to Katoomba on the train."

"OK. Well, maybe you could call me back within the month next time I call you. It would mean a lot to me. I worry when I don't hear back from you."

"Ah Allegra, I think you are happiest when you have nothing to do with me."

"That's not true. I'd love for us to have a more normal and less strained relationship."

"Hmmm well, we'll see. Maybe you could visit me sometime. Bring that nice boyfriend, but don't bring that horrible Justin."

"As if I would bring Justin, Mum!"

"Anyway, I have to go."

"See you." She was already striding away.

I went back to the shop feeling rather flat. Fortunately it was dead quiet for both Cherie from the beauticians and the bookshop, so Cherie came over and gave Lucie and me manicures.

There is nothing like a manicure and a good gossip with your friends to lift your spirits.

They were beyond excited to get the latest Teddy update and insisted I book in for a facial and leg wax on Friday.

"You want to look glowing and gorgeous Ally. You should have a body scrub too."

Apparently, unless I sloughed away some dead skin it was never going to work between Teddy and me. I had a feeling it was going to take more than that but I guess that was as good a place to start as any.

I didn't hear from him during the day and I knew that I should be OK because he had told me as much, but still, I was a bit nervous. A little old SMS would have been nice.

Naturally I also fielded calls from Caroline and Lisa. There are some things too fabulous and delicious to share in an email.

I also headed out for a big fat de-brief with Justin over lunch.

The unanimous view seemed to be that things looked good for a spectacular whirlwind romance if nothing else.

"Look, Ally, he could have just let it go, and that would have been the easiest thing", Justin said while picking at his Caesar salad. "He seemed like a great guy and he did seem to really like you."

"But what if it doesn't work out?"

"Then you've had some fun. If you can recall what that is?"

"What do you mean?"

"Listen sweetie, nobody loves you like I do, so I'm not afraid to say this. You have spent the time since you broke up with that last loser hanging out at the shop and doing not much else."

"I have a social life."

"Ally, you have friends but you do NOT have a social life."

"There is a difference?" Who knew there even was a difference?

"Of course there is. A social life is dinner parties, vacations and meeting new people. It's dancing and movies and last minute catch-ups. It is not coffee on a Saturday and drinks once a month when your friends can see you in between their own social life." Ouch.

"It's not that bad!"

"It is, you know. But this is your chance to go for it."

I wasn't so sure I wanted to "go for it" but I certainly didn't want to be that girl Justin was describing. I didn't think I was that girl, but I didn't want to turn into her either.

But the question I didn't ask Justin was "What do I do if it does work out?" How do I deal with that?

It was about 5.30pm and I was just starting to get things ready for closing. In the end it had been such a quiet day that I had let Lucie leave early.

The door did that little tinkle that it does when someone comes in and I looked up to see Louisa, Teddy's Louisa, or should I say Teddy's former Louisa, standing in my shop. She looked magazine editor fabulous in a pair of strappy pink heels and a pink and white striped jersey wrap dress. Her hair was perfectly neat and, despite it being about 100 degrees outside, she looked like she hadn't noticed, let alone perspired.

"Ah Allegra," she said as an opening.

"Hey, Louisa, what brings you to my little corner of the world?" It seemed a fair question.

"I'm just checking out the competition."

"There's a competition?" That was news to me. I thought she and Teddy were through.

"Well now," she was really eyeballing me, "there just might be".

"Oh." There seemed to me to be little else to say but she kept staring at me expectantly until she finally averted her gaze and looked around the shop.

"This is a cute little shop." It must have pained her to say something nice.

"Thanks."

"Not much of a career path though. That explains your attraction to Teddy and all the celebrity trappings. Must look like an easy way out."

Here we go.

"Actually, Louisa, the celebrity stuff is a turn-off, if you must know. And I love my shop, so getting out isn't part of my plan." Quite feisty for me.

"You own this shop!"

"I do."

Her brows arched at me. "That's surprising? I didn't pick you as being an entrepreneurial spirit."

"Well it's not like you even know me." And upon reflection it occurred to me that last time she'd seen me I'd been heading to the hospital, thanks to her. Under the circumstances I thought she could have been a little more conciliatory.

"Listen, I'm not here to get to know you."

"Really?" That was shocking news! "And I'm guessing you're not here to buy a book either."

"Look I'm sure you are a pleasant diversion for Teddy but listen to me - I have been with him for eight years and I have built his career every step of the way so I'm not about to just let him fly off to LA and international stardom and leave me behind. You need to know I'm not giving up easily."

If nothing else I admired her honesty. And I noticed there'd been no mention of the word love...

"Well, Louisa, if you think you have the power to make Teddy's decisions for him go ahead and use it. I know only one thing about men and that is that they always do exactly what they want. I am sure Teddy will be no exception."

She didn't look too pleased with my answer but she did take it as her cue to leave.

I guess I had more spirit than she bargained for.

***

I was dozing off to sleep that night when I got an SMS from Teddy.

Looking forward to Saturday. Miss you. T xxoo

At least he was thinking of me but I couldn't help but wondering if Louisa was SMSing him too or worse if he was SMSing her.

CHAPTER NINE

Justin stayed with me all week and every time I saw him I couldn't help but wonder about what he said.

Had I been shutting myself off? Was I really isolated? I had long felt like I had a nice circle of friends and finally, a sense of belonging. Still when someone says something like that to you it is hard not to see only the negative and feel suddenly you're not central to your friend's lives but really you're just on the periphery, of their lives.

You know instead of feeling content about your lot you feel like a hanger on. When I was at a book club that night I kept thinking, maybe these lovely people would prefer I wasn't here telling them what I thought of "Cloudstreet".

When I was talking to Lucie, I kept thinking that I shouldn't hold her up and I should let her go early so she could see her real friends, so she didn't feel she had to hang with her boss.

It's a weird thing how one person's opinion can mess with your head.

On Thursday at the next bridesmaid dress fitting, I brought it up with Lisa. I met her for a coffee beforehand. She was all wedding, which was to be expected, but she did make an extreme effort to ask about Teddy.

"This is so exciting Ally. It's so romantic."

"He has called me the past two nights and he even sent me more flowers. The apartment was so overwhelmed I had to take some downstairs. All the regulars in the shop were thrown. I'm not famous for floral arrangements down there. He's at some celebrity fundraiser tonight so we won't be talking."

"How exciting! Did you tell him about Louisa's visit?"

"No, I figured it was up to her." I wasn't sure if I had made the right decision but I didn't want to highlight the fact she was chasing him.

"So, tell me what are you doing Saturday for your big date, Ally?'

It was a secret. Teddy was planning the date and so I wasn't to know until it happened. It was very Hollywood I thought, but I was prepared to roll with that. Lisa was thrilled. She and I were the not-so closet romantics of the group.

I decided to ask her outright about my social life and my life in general.

"Lisa, Justin said something that got me thinking…"

"Yeah, Justin will do that." True enough. The girls loved Justin but we all knew he was very forthright.

"He said I have no social life and implied I am a virtual shut-in."

"Well, I think that is a bit harsh!" OK but she didn't totally refute it. "It's just that after the last boyfriend and your mum…well, you just seemed to lose all confidence."

"Really? Well, it was pretty bad."

"Look Ally, I agree. It just seems that since then you just stopped taking chances, you know getting out there and meeting people. And you were really never that adventurous to begin with."

"That's easy for you to say, you've been dating the same guy since you were 17." It was true; she had never taken a chance herself.

"I know, I have been incredibly lucky and I don't discount that." I guess that depends on whether or not you want to marry an accountant. "Look, all I'm saying is that it's great that Teddy came to you, however it turns out. But I have a good feeling about it."

"You haven't even met him."

"True, but he sounds nice from what you say. And I have seen him on TV so

I feel like I know him." She gulped down the last of her coffee. "Oh look we're late, let's go or mother will start lecturing the girls again! Poor Caroline!"

"So Ally, have you decided, are you going to ask him to the wedding?"

Hmm, good question.

Teddy called unexpectedly late that night and I really listened to him and I have to say I can see why he made it in TV because he has a deep, soothing voice. It was clear in that moment how women would love listening to him talk about pruning their hydrangeas and men would happily take paving advice from him.

It occurred to me that I still had never seen him on TV.

"You know I've still never watched your show. Do you want me to?"

"Not really. I mean it's cool either way. I wouldn't want you to compromise your principles."

"It's not a principle thing, exactly. Anyway, I just feel kind of bad; I mean you've been to my work."

"Ally, that's different." He paused to bite into his hotel club sandwich. He'd been too busy being Master of Ceremonies at the fundraiser to eat. They'd raised $1 million over the dinner. Amazing.

"But you've given me a great idea."

"What's that?"

"You should come to work with me one day next week."

"Really?" I couldn't imagine myself on a TV set. "That is your great idea?"

"Yeah it would be excellent. Then you can see what I do."

"Well, let's see how our first date goes," I suggested.

"OK," he laughed "But if we have a great weekend, will you promise to come?"

"I promise, but no pet segments. Do you do pet segments?"

"Sometimes."

"Well, I'm OK with cats and fish, just not dogs."

"We do have a cast dog, but I'll keep him away from you. I promise!"

Frankly the idea of both the dog and the shoot made me nervous but I couldn't think of a way to wriggle out of it.

My Friday was spent being primped and preened by Cherie in the beauty shop. I was waxed and scrubbed to within an inch of my life.

"Look Cherie, for all I know we're going bush walking!"

"That doesn't mean you can't start out with perfect skin and toenails."

Sometimes there is no point arguing with a professional trying to do their job.

It did feel nice but all the preparation made me really nervous. I'd never really felt nervous with Teddy before, except maybe at the party, because I hadn't been too sure if he liked me or not.

Now that I knew he did, well, it just felt like a much bigger deal. I really wanted him to like me but I was worried about what would happen if I let myself get close to him and he moved away. I just wasn't sure I wanted my heart broken again.

CHAPTER TEN

Teddy asked me to meet him at his place at 11am. A lunch date. Who doesn't like a long lunch?

"I know for a real first date I should pick you up, but it will work better this way."

"Is this just a ploy to get me to stay over at your place?"

"Maybe."

"OK, well I am not sure how I feel about that but I appreciate your honesty."

"You can't blame a guy for trying." True enough.

It's always hard to know what to wear when you don't know what you are doing.

My only instruction was "no stilettos". I wasn't planning on wearing them anyway but that was good to know.

I arrived at Teddy's punctually at 11am. It had been a very long morning of anticipation so, I figured, why draw it out.

It happened to be an extraordinarily hot day. It was one of those really warm February days that are rather exhausting and also rather fabulous, if you happen to like the heat, which I do.

I was wearing a blue flowing dress and some sparkly sandals. My hair was out except for a pretty blue clip securing it behind my right ear. I wore it out because I thought I might need to don a hat later and I didn't want bad hat hair.

Teddy opened the front door in casual taupe pants and a loose white linen shirt that showed off his lovely tan. He was as yet shoeless.

"Hey, Allegra." He gave me a welcoming hug and a lovely long kiss as he dragged me across the threshold.

"Hi."

"Are we ready to go?" He had keys on the front table.

"Ready if you are."

Then he ran to the kitchen and came back with two cold bottles of water and slid on his shoes.

"Great let's go."

"Where to?"

It turned out we were going for a walk. A lovely long walk over the Sydney Harbour Bridge, to be precise. It was a stroll from his place to the northern pylon and from there we could cross over to the city.

"I love walking across the Bridge and I thought we could work up an appetite for lunch."

"Great idea." It occurred to me I was walking across an Australian icon with an Australian icon, but I thought I'd keep that to myself.

Actually there weren't too many people out walking, I think because of the heat. We just strolled along, holding hands and chatting.

"So, Ally, is Justin still staying with you?"

"Yep. He's off to visit his Dad tomorrow but then he'll be back for Lisa's wedding in a couple of weeks."

"Ah, the wedding, got a date yet?"

"Still working on it. The hen's day is next weekend. I'm not big on hen's days, so I just have to keep reminding myself it's not about me."

"Sadly, I've never had the pleasure of attending a hen's day, but I have been to more than enough buck's nights to last me a lifetime."

"You don't like them?"

"The beginnings are fine. Not such a fan of the messy endings. The last one I went to the groom broke his arm."

"If I was the bride I would not be thrilled."

"I'm sure if you were the bride it wouldn't happen."

"Why do you say that?"

"I have a feeling you would pick someone a bit more respectful of you than that, given your love of chivalry."

"Indeed". I could not believe he remembered the chivalry conversation we'd had over our first drinks. "If I ever get married I hope you're right."

The Harbour was sparkling below us and ferries were busily taking people to and fro. It was a perfect day. When we got to the Rocks we went for a coffee in a cute café.

I was glad to be among the cool stone of the old buildings because it was getting pretty darn hot.

"So as this is our first date Mr. Green, maybe you should tell me a bit about yourself."

"Like what?"

"Well I really don't know too much about you except that you grew up in Bathurst, have three brothers and an ex-girlfriend, maybe more. You work on a TV show and are trained in landscape design...there are plenty of gaps, you know."

"I suppose so. I guess it's a TV thing that I'm quite private."

"I think you'll find it's a guy thing."

"You're probably right." We sipped our lattes. "OK ask me anything."

"OK. Why landscape design?"

"Well I wanted to do something where I got to work with my hands. And work outside - I hate being cooped up. I wanted to be part of a small team, and I had a good eye for design. Also I liked plants so it all kind of came together."

"Cool. So do you still do client work or just the TV?"

"Why? Are you going to do a roof garden in your building?"

"Well, I could...but no, I'm just curious."

"Some clients." Sip of coffee. "Would the owners let you do that?"

It seemed like a good time to come clean. "I am the owner. I own the building, the shop, the arcade, the lot."

"Wow, Ally." To know Sydney is to know that Sydney-siders are a people well versed in real estate values. It's a local obsession. I could tell he was doing some rough mathematical calculations in his head. "That's pretty amazing...I kind of thought..."

"I was a ditzy hippy shop girl..."

"Not that exactly, but..."

"Well, you know, I don't think it's a good idea to share with people the fact that I am a real estate mogul, it kind of changes things sometimes." I thought I'd hold back on the details of the other things I owned and how I came to own them for now.

"Fair enough. So you work in the shop because..."

"I love it more than anything!"

We were lunching at a harbourside restaurant so Teddy called us a water taxi. I'm usually a girl who takes the ferry so it was kind of fun!

"I would normally take the ferry too, but it's a first date and I'm trying to impress you". He said after booking the taxi. "How am I doing?"

"Not too bad so far."

"Excellent." He pulled me in close and kissed me while we waited for the taxi. "How about now?"

"Even better now."

Lunch was at a very groovy restaurant that perched over a pool and under the northern pylon of the Harbour Bridge.

It was one of those fabulous restaurants where only fabulous people come to eat.

As I was with one of the fabulous people I guess we passed muster.

It was very romantic sipping wine and watching the Harbour sparkle and bustle with ferries and pleasure boats. Sydney is a hard city to beat for natural beauty when it comes down to it.

I am not one of those girls who goes out on a date and pretends not to like food. I mean, seriously, I don't see the point. You are in a great restaurant with a world class chef preparing your meal, so why order a plate of leaves? I love leaves, for the most part, but I love seafood and steak and all manner of other beautifully prepared dishes more.

So we ordered up big! I had a starter of stuffed zucchini flowers and he had a plate of very plump and extremely delish oysters.

For main I had grilled snapper on a bed of asparagus risotto that was heavenly, and Teddy went for a yummy rack of Tasmanian lamb.

We started with some lovely Semillon and moved onto dessert wine with a shared dessert plate. He insisted on the shared dessert because he argued we were both full and also it was more romantic.

"It's a date after all, Ally."

During lunch we decided to play the 'What's your favourite?' game. You know that game where your list your top five favourite songs, movies, books or TV shows.

"This seems a little silly, baby" he objected initially.

"Of course it does, now what are your five favourite songs of all time?"

We didn't make it too far because we were too busy eating and drinking but we did establish a few things. For example Teddy's favourite ice-cream flavour is mango, and his favourite food is the Tim Tam. I also learned that the place he most wanted to visit that he never had was India and he learned that mine was Disneyland or Disneyworld. I'm not a Disney snob though obviously Euro Disney or the newly established Hong Kong Disney would not count.

"Disneyland? Why there?"

"Well, this sounds silly but to me I associate it with where nice normal, functional families go on their big vacation with their kids. I know obviously, not everyone goes, especially not from Australia but it just seems like if I make it to Disneyland then I won't be this weird hippy chick anymore."

"Fair enough. For the record I don't think you're a weird hippy chick." He kissed my fingertips.

"Thanks."

"And hey, if, or when, I'm in LA perhaps you'll get to Disneyland."

"We'll see." Gulp wine. "How are the talks going?"

"It looks like it'll be a goer. I'll find out and then basically bam I go because if it's not me it's another guy and they are all in place to start."

"It's a big move."

"Sure. If I fail I'll be done here too, I think…so it's a risk."

"Why would it fail?"

"TV is very fickle, baby. Maybe the US audience won't respond to me the way the Australian ones do."

"Come on, the accent gets you half way there already, plus you're hot, so I think, you'll do great."

"You think I'm hot?"

"Ah Mr. Green, would I be sitting here otherwise?"

"I suppose not," he said spooning some brulee from the dessert plate into my mouth and kissing me as a follow-up.

We strolled out of the restaurant and I was very glad we had walked before hand because I felt incredibly full and rather ditzy from the wine.

He pulled me towards Luna Park, the small old-fashioned amusement park under the northern leg of the Harbour Bridge. The entry is a large laughing clown face that you walk through.

"I've never been here."

"Really?"

"It was closed down when I first moved to Sydney."

"Well, Ally, today is your lucky day."

He lined up and got tickets while I freshened up. In my cubicle I could here a couple of teenagers talking about Teddy.

"Did you see Teddy Green out there, oh my God!"

"Oh my God, he is so gorgeous. I can't believe it!"

"Even cuter than on TV."

"Yeah, who was that chick he was with?"

"I don't know her, she must not do TV. I wonder how she met him, lucky cow. He sure is slumming it."

Nice. I stayed in the cubicle till I was sure they were gone.

Teddy was outside signing autographs for them when I came out. They looked at me a bit sheepishly when they realised I'd come from the loo, and then tossed their hair over their shoulders, fluttered at Teddy and left.

"You'll be pleased to know Teddy that those girls also think you are hot!" He blushed. That was kind of endearing. "Teddy, you don't think sixteen-year-old girls watch your show because they like flowers, do you?"

"I guess not." Good guess. "Come on lets go kiss on top of the Ferris wheel."

Now that is a plan you don't say no to. And this date was getting decidedly Hollywood.

***

So by the time we headed back to Teddy's it was late afternoon. I, for one, was feeling rather dreamy and relaxed. Nothing like drinking wine on a summer afternoon to make a girl a bit dozy.

Walking into Teddy's place was weird because I could feel Louisa's presence. The starkness and the clean lines were here all over.

"Are you OK, baby?"

"Yes, it's just, I don't know, this place doesn't seem very you."

He looked around. "Well you haven't seen upstairs, it's very me." He winked.

"I'm too nervous to ask."

"Well, no hurry and no need to be nervous. I'll show you later."

We walked through to the kitchen and tossed his keys on the bench. He went and unlocked the door to the courtyard and I strolled out. It seemed more relaxed than inside. Stylish but not stylised, if that makes sense.

"Are you happy with the garden, Teddy?"

"Today I am." He pulled me close and started kissing me. Part of me was very apprehensive that we were getting into this here. I mean so much privacy and I wasn't sure how far I really wanted things to go, as this was our first official date. But it was so nice and his arms around me felt divine.

He broke away. "Shall I get you a drink?"

"Sure, but don't forget, I will need to drive home." Good to at least act like you had some parameters.

"I know."

I sat down on an aubergine cushion on the edge of a water feature that was also a small fishpond filled with carp. It was kind of like mock seating.

He came back and handed me a wine. He sat really close.

"So tell me, Ally, what shall we do for the rest of the afternoon?"

"I do enjoy a good game of scrabble." He laughed and his baby blues sparkled. "Oh and backgammon, I'm great at backgammon."

"Baby, I'm sure you are." He kissed me again. "Cheers to a great first date!"

"Cheers." Our glasses clinked and we proceeded to kiss again.

And I guess we were pretty into it, because the next thing I knew out of the corner of my eye I saw fur and then a dog lunging towards us. Then I guess my instincts kicked in and moved backwards.

For future reference, it is not a good idea to move backwards when you are sitting on the edge of a water-feature because unfortunately you end up in it.

There was a loud splash. I was in the pond, the dog was on Teddy, and leaning in the doorframe was Louisa. I was really beginning to dislike her.

"Hope I'm not interrupting," she smirked.

Teddy had the dog by the collar. "Sit, Muffin, Sit! Ally, are you OK? Louisa, what the hell are you doing in my house again?"

"Gee, Teddy, that's no way to greet an old friend." She appeared to be thoroughly enjoying herself.

Teddy grabbed the dog, which was an Old English Sheep dog, and tied him up across the courtyard. Then he came back to fish me out of the pond. I must say the real fish looked relieved.

"Are you OK, baby? God I'm so sorry."

"I'm alright, just a little wet, I guess."

He sat me on a nice chair and then turned on Louisa.

"You come in here and talk to me now!" He grabbed her by the arm and dragged her into the kitchen. Not in a violent way, just in a "move you butt woman" kind of a way.

I figured that her behavior was not endearing in a "win back the guy way" so I figured she so must be going with the "if I can't have him no one can" approach.

He came out and gave me a towel.

"I'm so sorry about this, Ally; Louisa will be gone in a minute." He looked both furious and disappointed, which is a hard look to manage. He threw some biscuits to the dog who woofed them down, as dogs do.

"Why don't you just sip your wine and I'll be right back."

He went back in the kitchen and I heard raised voices but could not make out what was said. I tried to dry my butt and decided it was a lost cause.

The dog finished up his biscuits and promptly fell asleep. I wished I could do the same.

I also wished I could hear what Teddy and Louisa were saying.

It struck me that while we'd indeed had a fantastic day; maybe I wasn't really up for a fight to keep Teddy, when I wouldn't be really keeping him anyway, because he was going away in a few weeks as far as I knew. It kind of seemed a futile pursuit, as I'd no intention of moving to LA.

I sipped my wine and thought some more.

On the other hand I really didn't like Louisa's attitude and Teddy was a sublime kisser and good fun, so in that sense, maybe it was worth it.

Teddy came out and untied the dog. I saw him walk it through the house and out the front door and I saw Louisa follow. I heard the door slam and saw him coming back. He looked like thunder.

"Hey." I handed him his wine.

"Hey yourself." He sipped it.

"Do we want to talk about what just happened?" It seemed a fair question.

"Not just yet."

"Is Muffin the same dog that introduced us the other week?"

He nodded. I decided that Muffin wasn't all bad.

I guess he needed time to collect himself so we sat there quietly for a moment. Each of us was no doubt considering our next move.

"You're all wet. Do you want to change?"

"I'm not one of those girls who carry a spare outfit in her handbag." I supposed maybe Louisa was.

"I'm sure I can find something." He was warming up.

"Don't take this the wrong way but I have no intention of wearing anything of Louisa's."

"Why ever not? No, silly, I meant something of mine."

Well that could be cool. "Follow me."

"You are determined to get me upstairs one way or the other, huh?"

He turned over his shoulder and winked at me.

CHAPTER ELEVEN

Walking up the stairs it occurred to me that if I kept going there would probably be certain expectations that it would be hard to extricate myself from once I hit the top.

I just have a view point that it's not a great idea to go get changed in a guy's bedroom if you are not sure you want to be following through with that.

It occurred to me that even though I really did want to be with him that maybe for me, anyway, it would be a really, really bad idea.

After all, in the past two weeks his supposed ex-girlfriend had not only assaulted me, she had tracked me down at work and now set her dog on me.

I thought about how even if Teddy was doing his best to make a clean break from Louisa, and protect me, that he was in fact doing a pretty lousy job of that.

None of this in any way discounted the way I felt about him, or how much I knew I would enjoy myself if I made it to bed with him. And it really had been a while for me so that was something else to consider. I didn't want to blow the opportunity forever.

Plus I'd had all that waxing done. And I didn't want to have gone through all that for nothing.

It was a lot to think about so, because it wasn't a very big staircase, I decided to sit down half way up.

I was glad the stairs weren't carpeted because I was still pretty damp and made a wet squishy sound as I sat.

Teddy reached the top and turned around, I guess to see my back.

"Allegra?"

"Yes."

"Are you OK?"

"I was just having a little think."

He came back down and sat next to me on the step and held my hand.

"This afternoon hasn't gone quite like I expected, you know, baby?"

"I know." Still thinking.

"I'm really sorry about you know…"

"The whole pond incident? As it shall henceforth be known." I smiled at him.

"Yes, the pond incident."

"Here is my dilemma. I don't want to mess "this" up, but even more than that, I don't want to mess me up anymore than I already am."

"I don't want that either, baby." He put his arm around my shoulder and hugged me close. He felt warm and solid.

"And I think there's great potential for me to get seriously messed up by all this, whether you want it or not."

"OK, so how about we just don't do stuff to mess you up." That sounded pretty simple in theory but, the reality might be different.

"OK, well, that would include, uhmm you know, not you know".

It clicked with him. "Ah this is about "you know"?"

"Well, partly, but not entirely."

"Ok, now I'm catching on. Well, let's just take that out of the equation for a while."

"Really?"

"Sure" he replied, as if it was the simplest thing in the world. He grabbed my hand and pulled me up. "Now come on. Since we have established I'm not going to jump you, at least for today, let's get you some clean dry clothes before you leave a water stain on my beautiful new stairs."

The upstairs at Teddy's was quite different from the stark downstairs. It was more of a traditional terrace style with a couple of little staircases jutting off in different directions.

His bedroom was actually quite cozy, although it had a balcony with a killer view out over Sydney Harbour. It was chocolate brown walls with what looked like that suede effect paint, blonde wood and a cream and blue doona cover and lounge. It was male without being too testosteroney.

I went out on the balcony and looked out across the Harbour while he opened up a closet and found me a dry t-shirt and shorts.

I walked to the end of the balcony and saw that down the side of his house he had a lap-pool. I had read about how these were all the rage but I had never actually had met anyone who had one.

"You have a lap-pool." I called to him.

"I know." He stepped out on the balcony to meet me. "A little much you think?"

"You're asking me? What do I know about such things? I live over a shop, for goodness sake. I'm more olde world than modern design."

"I do use it. But it does seem a bit pretentious. I kind of got talked into it."

"Well, you know, it's there now so you may as well enjoy it, but that is an expensive thing to get talked into. Sometimes I get talked into a top I don't need and that's enough to make me tense."

"Well next time if you bring your swimmers we can take a dip." He handed me the dry clothes.

"As a matter of fact I have swimmers in the van. No dry clothes, of course, but I do have swimmers." He looked surprised. "Teddy, its summer and I live at the beach. You have to be prepared."

"OK then maybe later we can have a dip? "

"Maybe."

"The bathroom is through there if you want to change."

"Thanks." I noticed he'd kind of stepped back since we'd come upstairs. I hoped it was just a respect thing, not an "I wish she'd just leave now thing."

The bathroom was all tiny mosaic tiles and looked very like a Roman bath with that stony look. It was very male.

I turned on the shower for a quick, get the fishpond off me, rinse.

Naturally, while the shower was running, I did what all women do in this situation; I opened his bathroom cabinet. OK, we all know it's not right but a girl has to know some stuff about her guy. Favourite cologne, deodorant and toothpaste for starters. Also, in my case, I was looking for any lingering evidence of his recalcitrant ex.

There were all the usual things. Condoms, cotton buds, many male face creams, even some Clearasil. I found that comforting, it was good to know the man was not as perfect as he looked. The only womanly influence seemed to be an old lipstick...nothing that smacked of a current relationship anyway.

As I pulled on Teddy's t-shirt I noticed that the man had great smelling laundry. I am not good at laundry. Mine just never comes out as springy and fresh smelling as I wish it would. My friend Lisa and I use the exact same laundry products, because I use what she tells me to, and her clothes look great and smell like a garden, and mine smell like nothing and look like they've been washed a hundred times. Teddy's laundry smelt like Lisa had been over helping him out. I made a mental note to call her and check up on that later.

That got my mind thinking about Lisa's wedding. It was now two weeks away and if he went away, Teddy would be leaving the day after the wedding.

I wondered if I should invite him. There were so many issues to consider. Firstly would he want to spend the day before he left with me? Secondly would he even have time? Thirdly would we still be together by then? Fourthly, did I want to spend the day before he left me, with him and in such a public place, with everyone I knew staring at us? Too many things to consider. The easy option was, of course, not to take him because Justin was going anyway and he and I could be each other's handbags as usual. Just thinking about it made my head hurt, so I decided to stop.

When I came out of the bathroom Teddy has changed out of his "lunch clothes" into a baby blue t-shirt and shorts. The baby blue shirt really brought out the colour of his eyes and made them almost iridescent. I wondered if he knew that and was using an unfair advantage.

"Hey, you took your time."

"Sorry. Do I get the rest of the tour now?"

"Baby, you can have anything you want." OK Allegra, get yourself out of the bedroom.

"Great, I'll take the tour then."

It turned out that Teddy had a whole upstairs room that was like a home theatre. The big humungous wide screen TV with all that surround sound or whatever it was called.

The room was cool and dark and seemed to me totally at odds with the sultry summer day outside.

And he also had a killer movie collection. I'm a sucker for old Hollywood movies. There is nothing like a Cary Grant or Hepburn and Tracey movie to while away an afternoon. I flicked through his collection.

"These are great. How come you have so many old ones?"

"I just like them."

"You don't just have them here to impress chicks?"

"Do you think that would work?"

"Seriously, it might." I winked at him. "Not on me of course, but you know, some of the other weaker girls might fall for it."

"I'll keep that in mind."

"Why don't we watch something?"

"Sure why not? It's a while till our evening plans."

"We have evening plans?"

"Baby, I promised you a memorable date."

We sat down together on the plush sofa and began to watch Adam's Rib.

Chapter Twelve

The next thing I knew I was alone in a dark empty room, sprawled out across the sofa and the movie had ended.

I must have been seriously affected by the wine and fallen asleep. I really hoped I hadn't snored or drooled on him.

How embarrassing to fall asleep halfway through a date. Though I suppose it's a compliment that I was that relaxed.

Then again how dull and weird did it make me seem?

I bet Louisa never fell asleep on a date.

I had no idea what time it was. Teddy had wandered off at some point, the excitement of my company clearly being too much to handle.

I surely knew how to show my appreciation for a great date, didn't I? I wished I was the sort of gal who carried a mobile phone with her at all times so I could phone a friend and ask what the etiquette was in such situations, but then again who would be so foolish to have had a similar experience?

There was really nothing to do but head out into the house and find the lovely Teddy.

***

Downstairs smelled of grilled meat. It smelled like barbeque.

I ambled through to the kitchen area where Teddy was madly chopping salad greens.

The whole back of the house was lit by candles and it looked very dreamy and romantic.

"Hey, sleepy-head!" He looked up from his task affectionately.

"Sorry I feel asleep. I'm a bit embarrassed."

"It's cool. We'll blame the wine."

He was back chopping.

"So what are you up to?"

"I'm just making some dinner."

"It smells great. Can I help?"

"Yes, you can sit there and look decorative." That was quite the ask in his clothes with my bed-head in action. "Listen, I do want to apologise about the pond incident this afternoon."

"I'm not entirely sure you and Louisa have closure, Teddy." I am quite skilled in the art of understatement.

"Well, I have closure, but she is very determined to get what she wants."

"And she wants you!"

"No, I don't think that's it. She hasn't really wanted 'me' for a long time. I think she wants to be part of some imagined celebrity couple. She broke it off, you know?"

"I didn't."

"She was right to do so. Her reasons for the break-up were wrong but she was right."

"What were her reasons?" Of course I was curious.

"They don't matter now. And honestly I like Louisa, I know you haven't seen her at her best but she is a smart, motivated person. She is just a bit lost at the moment. We should have broken up a few years back, but you know how sometimes relationships just become a habit..."

"I haven't had a long-term one to speak of."

"That's hard to believe. You're just fussy huh?" He looked so earnest.

"Hmmm, maybe not fussy. Maybe cautious or wary is a better word."

"What's there to be wary of?" Was he serious?

"Teddy, it's a tough old world out there for the non-celebrities."

"Well, I guess I haven't really been out there much, dating."

"You'll be alright, anyway. You're a smart, good-looking guy with an Aussie accent. Those LA chicks will be all over you."

"I hope not. I hope you'll be with me and that would be rather inappropriate in your presence, don't you think?"

"Hmm, well, keeping in mind that I'm wary, let's just wait and see, but I do agree that if I'm there that should be discouraged."

"Listen, are you hungry or do you want to have a swim before dinner? It's pretty hot!"

It was one of those breezeless nights where a cool change would be welcome but it didn't feel like one would be showing up anytime soon.

A swim sounded good. And in the pool not the fishpond this time.

I grabbed my swimmers from the van and ran upstairs and got changed. I was quite thankful for all that waxing, scrubbing and scouring that had taken place the day before.

And I was also thankful that I'd allowed Lisa to talk me into buying a cute and glamourous 1950's screen-goddess-style swimsuit for the summer.

"If I had curves I'd be very proud of them," she had argued. Lisa was more you're straight up and down kind of a gal.

"Baby, you look amazing!" I guess Teddy liked the swimsuit too.

He wore Hawaiian print board shorts. Glad he wasn't in a Speedo at this point in proceedings.

He brought a champagne bucket out to the pool. All the lights were out except the ones inside the pool itself. It was tiled in clear blue mosaic tiles so it was like swimming in tropical waters by moonlight. I slid into the water and decided there were far worse ways to spend a Saturday night than hanging at Teddy's place.

"I think the lap-pool was a great idea!"

"Me too!" He said pulling me close. "It's unanimous."

"I thought we were cooling off."

"I think that is an unreasonable request given that killer suit."

"Sorry."

"Oh baby, please don't apologize."

After awhile we could smell the meat on the barbeque burning so Teddy extricated his limbs from mine and hopped out of the pool. I hopped out too and went to get changed. My own clothes were dry so I slid back into them and made a feeble attempt at fixing my make-up. I flipped my hair up with a clip that was floating in the bottom of my bag. I didn't look too bad for this late in the day.

Dinner was a delicious rosemary roasted lamb he did on the barbie and some great veggies all mixed together – eggplant, zucchini, squash. And of course potatoes, after all he was a guy.

We sat in the courtyard and chatted by candlelight.

It was all a little too perfect. Surely this guy had a massive flaw somewhere. Hopefully not.

He did admit he wasn't much of a reader, but then again I could have worked that out for myself.

"Although I do have my own book coming out this week. The book launch is Tuesday night."

"Really?"

"Yeah, do you want to come? It's a gardening book called *The New Green Garden*."

"Wow! That's impressive. Sure I'll come, unless I have bridesmaid commitments."

"OK, let me know." He leaned back in his chair. "You take your friendships very seriously, huh?"

"You think I shouldn't?"

"No, of course you should but…"

"I read a quote somewhere that said, "Friends are the family we choose for ourselves." It's a mantra for me. Those of us with less than perfect families have to do that, or be alone."

"Ah I see."

"And also those of us who aren't serial monogamists have to make more effort too."

"Serial what?" His left eyebrow shifted quizzically north.

"You know someone who isn't always in a long-term relationship. We don't have that fallback. For better or worse people in couples have each other to fill those empty times and to rely upon. I've never had that. I have friends."

"Sounds like the better deal, well if you are in the right relationship then maybe not."

It hit about 10pm and I was exhausted. We'd had some yummy strawberries in cointreau and an espresso coffee from the very shiny machine in Teddy's kitchen and I was seriously tired. Even he looked tired.

"I guess I should be making tracks."

"Really? Can't you stay?"

"Well I can but…"

"I'll be a good boy and only feel you up a little bit."

"Thanks Teddy, that's so comforting. Not!"

"Seriously, I want you to stay. I love having you here." How can you say no to that? I'm only human. Fair enough. It was taking me considerable restraint too.

Snuggling up in Teddy's big soft bed after a wonderful day together had a surreal feel to it. What was I doing here?

When I looked at him it just didn't make any sense. What was he doing with me? Sure I'm a great girl but the world is full of great girls and most of them it seemed to me didn't get this lucky.

Yet there I was in that sweet smelling bed next to that sweet smelling guy.

As we were drifting off to sleep I asked him;

"Hey Teddy, do you want to come and meet my friends at a lunch tomorrow?"

"Baby, I can't think of a better way to spend tomorrow. OK well, I can think of one way, but lunch will do fine."

CHAPTER THIRTEEN

I totally love my girlfriends but it's not because of their innate subtlety, I can assure you.

When I turned up to brunch with Teddy in tow they just about jumped up and down on the spot and clapped their hands like twelve-year-old girls.

If Teddy noticed, he didn't react. And frankly there was no way he couldn't have noticed.

He was very polite and played it cool while I introduced him to the girls and their partners, especially as they were wildly gesticulating and mouthing "Oh my God!" behind his back.

It occurred to me that if this was how fairly sophisticated women behaved in his company it must be rather bizarre when unsophisticated ones crossed his path.

It wasn't until I was dragged to the bathroom after about five minutes that I realised their reaction had nothing to do with him and that they would have behaved the same way had I brought any half decent fellow to a gathering. Apparently I had become such a dateless spinster that I could have brought a middle-aged balding schoolteacher and they still would have clapped and jumped. Well, that's what they said but I knew the hot factor contributed on some level.

"So, Ally, how was the date?"

"Where did you go?"

"Did you make it home?" Thanks Caroline.

"The date was great." I filled them in on the basics, minus the pond incident.

"Oh sweetie that sounds fantastic!" Lisa.

"Did you stay the night?" Again from Caroline.

"Yes, but nothing happened."

"Yeah right!" Caroline who was he the lustiest of the bunch was incredulous. She read my facial expression and saw I was telling the truth. "Are you nuts? What were you thinking? Please do not tell me he is gay. I can't bear for us to lose another good one."

"He's not gay! I just wasn't ready." I then told them about the pond incident.

"Good for you sweetie!" That was what I loved about Lisa; she always supported my choices, no matter how ill advised they seemed to the rest of the world.

"I would still have slept with him. After all he didn't invite Louisa over she just showed up."

"No, no she had to feel comfortable." Lisa again.

"Listen, shall we go have lunch? We can talk about this later." Caroline, always was practical.

Teddy and the boys were discussing some sport or other upon our return.

We were at the very famous Watson's Bay Hotel in Sydney's east. It is a pub with a beer garden and restaurant with the most spectacular view across the city. Unlike yesterday's posh lunch, this place was all about fish and chips, burgers and icy beers. It's a place where groups gather on sunny Sundays to waste the afternoon, catch up, or sample the hair of the dog after the night before.

The boys had gotten our drinks while we were gone so we had a toast to the happy couple, Lisa and Mike. This lunch was like a last hurrah before the true wedding madness of the next fortnight enveloped us.

"To the happy couple!"

"Cheers" Clink. Clink. Clink. Clink.

"So Teddy, are you coming to the wedding?" Lisa asked.

"Well she hasn't asked me," I heard him whisper back conspiratorially.

"Don't worry, she will."

"Well, Teddy is probably moving to LA that weekend, so he may well be a bit busy."

"Really mate, what have you got happening?" And then they were all ears as he told the guys about the "big deal."

"I'm hoping to find out this week. Of course I hope I get it, but either way now I just need to know."

"For sure."

Time to order so off trotted the guys. They were being all manly and getting extra drinks as well. Caroline had gone to the ladies again, this time for real.

"He seems lovely, Ally."

"Yeah, he is Lisa. He's really genuine, I think."

"He seems it."

We sipped our drinks.

"Honey I'm not one to give advice but I think you should go for it. It's better to have loved and lost, you know."

"Is it?"

"You know it is. And you might win."

"How can I win? The only way is if he doesn't get the job. And I can't wish that he fails, I want him to succeed."

"You could go to LA."

"No, I couldn't." As if? "And he hasn't asked me anyway."

"What if he does?"

"No guy is going to ask a chick he's been dating under a month to move to the States with him."

"He might."

"Lisa that just won't happen."

Everyone wandered back so we changed the topic. People kept saying hi to him by name or "Hey mate, great show."

No anonymity. He didn't seem to be overly bothered by it but it made me feel very self-conscious when he was leaning in close or touching me…as if people were watching me. Because, of course, they were, though not maybe to the extent I imagined.

Its weird enough going out with your 'new boyfriend' with friends, let alone when the whole pub staring at you.

And then someone came over whom Teddy knew for real. It was the Lizard, the guy who had been hitting on Lucie at Teddy's party. He looked no less creepy. It was a hot day and he was wearing a black turtleneck again. Maybe he was eternally trapped in the same top.

"Hey Green, how's it going mate?" Teddy stood and shook his hand.

"Good Nathan." It actually surprised me when he didn't call him The Lizard; I forgot it wasn't his real name. Teddy made the rudimentary introductions. "What brings you out here today?"

"Lunch with the ex and kids. Major drag. Saw Louisa last night at Bar Roomba. Not a pretty sight."

"Oh?"

"She was rather drunk but totally bad mouthing you. She's got a temper, that one. I tried to console her mate, but she wasn't having any of it. I took her back to my place but she wigged out on me. She's less fun when she's psycho, don't you think?"

I saw Teddy flinch at the thought of the Lizard with Louisa, or maybe it was the psycho reference. It upset me briefly but then I thought, I don't even like Louisa and I wouldn't want her consoling herself in the Lizard's slimy arms. Awkward silence followed.

"Well, Nathan, we won't hold you up. We were just about to eat."

"Oh right" It just then occurred to the Lizard that maybe he was talking to the wrong guy about this, or if not that, then in front of the wrong people. "Better get back to Attila, the ex."

"He seems nicer on TV." Thanks Lisa. "Less sleazy."

Apart from that I thought the lunch was a success. He really seemed to hit it off with the gang.

"See you at the wedding, mate," the guys kept saying as a farewell. Partly cause they liked him and also to get my goat.

"Hold onto that one," Caroline whispered in my ear as we left.

He drove me back to his place in the ute.

"You have lovely friends, Ally."

"Thanks, I think so."

"Not that I'm surprised." What a sweetheart. "Will you come in?"

"You know what? I think its time for me to head home."

"Scared I might draw you into my alluring web?"

"Frankly, yes."

"Baby, would that be such a bad thing?" He asked squeezing my hand.

"Not too bad at all. But I'm still going home."

My heart knew if I didn't leave then it might never get out in one piece.

"Well, I'll call you tomorrow."

Except he called me that night.

"Hey, are you still on to come to work with me this week?"

"If you want me to."

"What about Tuesday? I have a shoot for the TV show in the day and then the book launch. You can meet my mum and dad at that."

"Oh, well, I'm not sure I'm quite ready for that." In fact I was quite sure I was NOT ready for that!

"You will be fine. They'll love you. I'll get Jane, my assistant, you remember her? Anyway she'll call you and line it all up, OK?"

What could I say except, "Sure that would be great."

I supposed it was a good sign that he wanted me to meet his folks. Well, maybe...

Chapter Fourteen

Jane called me and told me to be at an address in Birchgrove at 11am on Tuesday. She gave me excellent directions and was super friendly.

"The book launch is at the Botanical Gardens so you can go on from the shoot. It will be tight because we have to finish the garden make-over and get Teddy to the evening event by 7pm. You'll need to bring a change of clothes. Have you got email? I'll email you the invite."

Great. First a shoot with builders and dogs, and then a book launch and meet the parents.

"There is no way to prepare for that," Lucie informed me when I hung up the phone. "The best thing you can do is just go with it."

"You think?"

"Sure I mean who has experience with that sort of thing? No one can help you. You just have to wing it."

Strangely I didn't find Lucie's advice overly comforting.

I found the street in Birchgrove, and what I also found was I couldn't get my car down it. Birchgrove is a small inner-city suburb made up of small streets lined with what were once workers cottages and terraces. In recent years, due to its proximity to the city, and the harbour, it has been totally gentrified. The street was one of those skinny two-way streets that really should be one-way. It was charming and terrace lined ordinarily, but, thanks to the TV truck, the landscaping deliveries and the extra people, it was chaos. I parked the Kombi about a mile away and hoofed it in.

Then I had to make my way past some security guys. After 10 minutes of grappling with them, I had to call Teddy on his mobile phone to get myself let in.

He came racing out to rescue me.

"Kevin, this is Allegra. She's with me."

"Sorry, mate, no one told me you had a new chick." And nice to meet you too, Kevin! Not a great start, I didn't think.

"Baby, I'm sorry. I thought it was all taken care of." He gave me a quick peck on the cheek as he dragged me around the back.

"That's fine. I just didn't want to interrupt you."

We found Jane and then Teddy raced off for a 'piece to camera'. Apparently that's one of the close-ups where he stands leaning on a shovel and talks directly to the camera, as if speaking to the home viewer personally.

Jane found me what was supposed to be an out-of-the- way nook to sit. The problem with backyards the size of envelopes, is that during a TV renovation show with cameramen, labourers, directors, lighting guys and delivery men, there are simply no out-of-the-way nooks.

There were about fifty 'excuse me's' and 'would you mind just moving over here love's' in the first 15 minutes. Apparently we were in the yard of a down-on-his-luck former Olympic swimmer, Bill "Digger" McAveny, who also had Parkinson's disease. Even with my scant knowledge of the inner workings of the television industry, I could tell that this episode would be a ratings winner.

I had never been on a TV set before so it was quite fascinating to watch how it all came together. And to see how many people are at work behind the scenes making these shows.

After an hour Jane rescued me and we went to get some coffee from the catering truck.

"So it seems to be going well with Teddy." It wasn't a question.

"I guess so."

"Listen, you wouldn't be here otherwise. I know Teddy. We've worked together 10 years." Interesting.

"So if he gets the US job, what happens to you?"

"I'll just run his Australian stuff. DVDs, books, speaking gigs when he comes back. It would be great for me. I've got kids I never see so I could work a whole lot less than I do now, but for the same pay." Seemed like it was a great deal for everyone but me." So will you go with him?" I nearly spat my coffee on her.

"What makes you think it's even a possibility?"

"Allegra, as I said, I know Teddy. He's an outgoing guy with mates and a life, you know. He is very likely moving away in a week or two, and yet he's spending all his time with you. He cancelled a ton of stuff to spend the weekend with you. It makes no sense unless he plans on being with you. If he wants a fling he can go and have that in LA." Uh oh.

"What kind of stuff?"

"Sorry?"

"What kind of stuff did he cancel?"

"Soccer with his mates. Dinner plans with friends. He even begged off a charity event. He never does that. He sent a hefty donation but still, he never skips stuff."

"Oh." I was feeling a little thrown by this information. I'd just assumed he was a bit of a loner, I guess, or maybe I hadn't thought about it enough. Obviously he had a life. I knew he had friends. I mean he had a house full of people at the party only two weeks ago.

"Don't freak on me, OK? It's a good thing." She patted me reassuringly on the arm. "He deserves a great girl. He's the best." Indeed he was. But was I the right great girl?

I quietly sipped my coffee while she fielded some phone calls and people whirred around us.

Maybe this was more serious than I thought.

"Come on, let's go back and watch some more."

I made it through the afternoon OK, although my head was spinning. It went pretty smoothly, I thought.

That was until the point when I had to climb on a director's chair to avoid the cast dog, Nigel, and the chair folded up beneath me. I toppled over on my ass on the semi-tiled porch, legs akimbo. I was glad I was wearing pants, not a skirt. It was not a highlight of the day. But on the upside, Nigel, thought I was a freak and moved away allowing me to breathe easy for the rest of the afternoon.

I'm sure everyone else thought I was a weirdo, especially as they were used to seeing Teddy with the oh-so-together Louisa, but Teddy himself seemed to find it a strangely endearing display.

He swooped over and scooped me up.

"Oh, baby, are you OK?"

"I'm fine. Just feeling ridiculous."

"No. I should have kept the dog away from you. I promised I would."

"Well you are kind of busy."

"I know but a promise is a promise. Anyway, if you're alright, I have to run, Digger is out the front."

It was strange watching the show work. Obviously Teddy wasn't the only one working on the show, but he was definitely treated like the star and he did seem to know what he was doing from a horticultural perspective as well. I knew he was qualified, but maybe I had assumed that his skill was secondary to his appearance as far as the television role was concerned. Very shallow of me, really!

I hid behind some burly builders when Teddy walked "Digger McAlveny" through to see his new yard. I could unobtrusively peer between their waists. "Digger" was old, and with the Parkinson's he was pretty wobbly, so Teddy had him by the arm and was guiding him.

"So, Digger, what do you think?"

"Bloody amazing, mate, bloody amazing!" That was all he could say. His daughter who had organised the whole thing went and hugged him. It was very emotional.

"Well, Digger, you've done so much for Australian swimming we just wanted to give something back." Teddy told him.

It was quite the misty moment all around.

Pretty soon the old feller was lying on a new teak recliner under some floodlights having an icy ale and Teddy was grabbing me and dragging me out to his car.

"That was great Teddy. He seemed so touched. What a nice thing to do for someone. It must be so rewarding."

"Some days. Where are you parked Ally?" Obviously there was no time for small talk. I told him where the car was.

"Let's swing by your car, grab your gear, and then we'll change at my place and head to town. Shit, we only have just over an hour."

"Why don't I drive myself?"

"My way will be faster."

"How do you know?"

Teddy pointed out that as I drove a 1970 combo and he drove a late model V8 ute that it was really a no brainer. Men and cars.

I decided not to argue and we were at his place by 6.15pm. It was a white-knuckle journey. Thank goodness we didn't get booked.

"Do you always drive like that?"

"Only on nights like these. Come on, Mum and Dad are waiting inside!"

Was he serious? I had expected to meet them at the book launch. Not now. Not here.

It was too late to ask him anything. He had my bag in his hand and was taking his front steps two at a time.

CHAPTER FIFTEEN

Meeting the parents is not one of my strong suits.

Having never had such a normal family myself, normal families make me very nervous. It's as if I feel they will take one look at me and know that bizarre hippies raised me and surmise that I don't fit in. I always feel I won't belong.

Justin thinks this is the most ridiculous of all my hang-ups. I discussed it with him over wine and dinner the night before when I heard I was to be meeting Teddy's parents.

"Sweetie, first of all you are boringly normal these days."

"Thanks, how reassuring."

"Secondly, you are adorable."

"OK, I like you again now."

"Good. Thirdly you are totally loaded, so any sane parent would be jumping for joy if you hooked up with their son." Eye roll. "And finally, people, even the normal straight-laced ones, are not as judgmental as you think. They don't think you should be cast aside because of loopy parents. It's not like wolves raised you, you know. They probably don't even think about your parents at all."

"Maybe you're right."

"When will you learn that I am always right? Now top up my wine!"

After more wine and a few mouthfuls of mushroom risotto he launched into some psychobabble about me self-sabotaging myself and kept repeating that if all

I want in life is to be normal, then surely joining or being accepted by a normal family should be my nirvana.

"Instead, Ally, you plan to skulk in there as if you have something to apologise for. That's not endearing. That won't win their hearts!"

"Very Hugh Grant with the skulking comment."

"Thank you, I try at all times to be as much like a character in one of those Four Weddings and Notting Hill movies, as I can." He was a nut, for sure. "Go in and be yourself. Teddy likes you for you, quirks and all. Let them see the real you, not the watered down version."

"Maybe you are right."

"As I said – when will you learn?"

So I decided to take his advice. Why, I don't know, because on reflection his love life was usually a bigger disaster than mine. I guess I just needed to take someone's advice and his got me out of the car and up to the front door where Teddy was calling out to his folks.

"Mum and Dad, we're here!" He sounded like an excited sixteen-year-old. Or maybe like a puppy would sound if puppies could in fact talk.

"We're back here Ted." His dad had one of those deep, stern fatherly voices that you expect from, well, fathers and especially those who are school principals.

I caught up with Teddy who grabbed my hand and I sort of slid through the house to the kitchen area.

His dad was a tall fairly good-looking man in his mid-sixties. He had a good head of hair and Teddy's eyes, without the sparkle. His mother was a tiny dot of a woman with a brunette bob, and totally different eyes from Teddy, but hers did have the twinkle.

"Mum and Dad this is Allegra. Ally, this is my mum and dad. Bob and Joyce Green."

Mr Green extended his hand and pleasantries.

Mrs Green swooped forward and hugged me.

"Darling I'm so pleased to meet you. Teddy has been singing your praises. Oh don't blush now. I'll get in trouble for having embarrassed you."

"Well, it's lovely to meet you."

"Son, we're going to be late. You'd better get a wriggle on."

"Yes, and you stink sweetie so you had better race and have a shower."

"Thanks mum!" He looked genuinely embarrassed. Funny how your mother can embarrass you know matter who you are.

"Well, wouldn't you rather know?"

"I'm sure that Ted knows when he stinks Joyce, he's a grown man."

"Sorry, you know it's hard to let go. It's a mother thing. I'll bet Allegra's mother is just the same." Teddy and I exchanged knowing glances.

"Right, well, I'll use the ensuite. You can use the other bathroom, Ally. OK? And change in the TV room. We have 15 minutes."

"We'll just sit here and drink your wine son." Go Mr Green. Perhaps he and Johno would get on after all.

"Sounds like a plan."

Twenty minutes later we were all in Teddy's car flying across the Harbour Bridge." Men in the front, ladies in the back.

"Slow down son, for goodness sake," Bob reprimanded him for going ninety in a sixty zone.

"So Teddy, sweetheart, who will we know at this event?" She turned to me, "Allegra we know some of Teddy's friends but not too many of the TV types. Of course I feel like I know them from watching the show. Last time I started talking to that carpenter chappy as if I knew him and he looked at me like I was a lunatic."

It seemed Joyce was the talker in the family.

"Mum, not too many friends are going; it's just a publicity thing. Guy is going and Mark. You'll know Jane of course." Teddy was pitching a hard left onto the Cahill expressway.

"Not to bring up anything sensitive, but will Louisa be there? I need to prepare myself because after last time…"her voice trailed away.

"She might be there." Teddy was eyeing me in the rearview mirror to gauge my reaction, which I kept remarkably neutral considering how I felt. "I'm really hoping she won't be, but I'm sure she would have been invited in her editorial capacity."

"Oh dear," sighed Joyce.

"Joyce!" I don't care what Bob thought. I was with Joyce and thinking - oh dear! We made it at 6.55pm and Jane was standing anxiously in the doorway.

"Thank God!" She quickly hugged Joyce and Bob and whisked Teddy away.

"Come on, ladies. Let's get ourselves a drink." I was really beginning to like Bob a lot.

"Do you come to many of Teddy's work things?" I thought I'd make the conversation with Joyce while Bob was at the bar.

"We used to. Then we stopped for a while." I thought she was going to say more but she saw Bob coming back. "But we missed Teddy and he's so busy it's about the only way to see him. And with him probably going away, we could hardly miss this."

"Well you must be very proud of him."

"We're proud of all our boys." Go Bob! He handed around the bubbly. "I'm proud of the fine men they've turned into. They are all different, but all fine men." I thought I was going to cry. I looked at Joyce and she was tearing up.

"We're so blessed." OK if this was what normal families were like I was feeling particularly ripped off about my childhood!

Then I saw Louisa out of the corner of my eye. She was wearing a very fetching hot pink dress with a low-cut front and ruffled hem. She was striking; I had to give her that.

I was wearing a beige dress and wondered in that moment what I had been thinking when I chose it. I knew exactly what I'd been thinking. Blend in. I knew I looked fine if not fabulous. I looked like who I was – a sweet girl from a bookshop and Louisa looked like who she was – a woman on a mission.

Louisa strutted over to our little group and I saw Bob pull himself up.

"Joyce. Bob. Always a pleasure." She gave them each an Arctic air kiss. And they politely leaned into receive it. "Allegra, still hanging around, I see?"

"Louisa!" Bob had his best principal voice on. Allegra is our guest and I would expect you to treat her accordingly." If it didn't work out with Teddy I thought maybe I could get Bob to adopt me or at the very least just be my bodyguard. Though I did have Johno and he might be offended if I got myself a new dad. Still it was tempting.

"Of course!" Her voice tinkled with benign contempt. "I haven't seen you two in ages. And what an exciting occasion! Teddy and I put so much work into this book. It really was a team effort." She caught sight of someone fabulous over my right shoulder and swanned off. "See you later."

"Horrid girl!"

"Joyce!"

"Look, Bob, I'm entitled to my opinion. I never liked her. I'm on record as never having liked her, you know that. The first time I met her, I said that. And as if she did a thing, even one thing, towards this book. She has some nerve."

"Let it go. It's water under the bridge, love."

"Is it? Look at her."

"Don't look at her, that's what she wants, the minx. Look at Teddy. He's with Allegra now and he's happy."

OK, now I really did want to cry. Good thing some fellow everyone else in the room recognised, no doubt from TV, took to the stage to start proceedings.

The fellow introduced Teddy in glowing terms and then he took his place at the podium looking very celebrity. It's funny how he almost didn't seem like my Teddy at all. It was if another confident, alpha-male inhabited his body when he was working, and my Teddy was this mellow, very cruisey guy by contrast. He did look extremely hot I thought. It was clear why women swooned over him. In fact near me a woman made some suggestive comments. If Joyce overheard, she didn't react.

His presentation about the book and its inspiration was brief but very passionate.

I hoped he one day discussed me with the same fervor that he exhibited when waxing lyrical about green urban corridors.

He thanked the network, the people he worked with and the editor, the photographer and especially Jane for their effort and support. He was finished and down signing books in a matter of minutes.

I noticed Louisa seething in the corner of the room, no doubt missing the accolades she was used to receiving at such events.

When it was over Bob went for another round of drinks and Guy the dude, whom I had met at Teddy's party, made his way over.

"Hey, Joyce!"

"Hello, Guy, how you are you sweetheart?"

"Cool. Ted did well, don't you think? Book looks good."

"It's lovely." Joyce was leafing through a copy.

"How is your head, Allegra? That was quite a scene."

"Fine thanks."

"What scene?" I don't know much about mothers but women cat fighting over their sons might not be seen as endearing to them.

"Oh nothing." And divert. "So what's new with you, Guy?"

Another guy called Mark joined us. It turned out Guy the dude, Mark and Teddy were uni buddies and had flatted together in Bondi for a few years. They were also part of the weekend soccer team that Teddy had ditched for me a few days ago.

"Well Ally, I would have ditched my mates for you too," said Dave sweetly. He was clearly on his umpteenth beer but I was happy with the sentiment anyway.

They seemed like nice guys. Mark was in banking. I'm not sure what part exactly. And Guy was in magazines. Turns out he was the editor of a surfing magazine. Totally fitted the Guy-the-Dude, image, I thought.

The evening seemed to progress OK. I saw Teddy and Louisa disappear into the garden for a while and that made me nervous. Even more so when she returned looking smug and triumphant and he returned looking sad.

Still, he slid straight back into working-the-crowd mode.

I did wonder why I was there, to be honest. I totally understood his need to work the room, but why I needed to stand there and watch was a bit of a mystery. It's extremely hard work making small talk for three hours with your new boyfriend's parents, especially when you know almost nothing about them.

We had covered such topics as gardening, the bookstore, how Manly has changed since the old days, Teddy's possible overseas move and the drought and its affect on rural Australia all by 9pm.

I was actively trying to avoid any discussion of my own non-nuclear family and my complicated history. Frankly, I was exhausted after an entire day of small talk. I talk too, in the shop obviously, but not to that extent. Small talk is not my thing.

When Joyce headed off to powder her nose Bob said to me conspiratorially "You're doing great, honey, only another hour to go."

"Oh, no, I'm having a lovely time."

"Allegra, how could you be? You are doing great, all things considered, but no one could be thinking you are having a lovely time". He sipped, "Well, no one but Ted. I'm not sure if that boy is being insensitive or optimistic this evening."

When he put it like that I just felt more tired.

Why was I here? What was the point? Couldn't I just go home? Maybe I could sneak out and hop on a ferry and no one would even know.

Teddy breezed by shortly after. "Hey, Ally, how's it going? You OK?"

"Sure. I'm fine."

"I should be done soon. Then we can go home."

"Actually I think I'll just head to my place."

"You are not coming back?" He was seriously incredulous.

"Not tonight."

"Let me take Mum and Dad home and drop you off, then."

"That's not necessary. You should spend some time with them."

Jane came up and called him away to talk to someone important so I hit the bathroom. Of course Louisa was in there.

"Having fun, Allegra?"

"Yes thanks. Are you? It's a lovely evening."

"I think so. I mean I know everyone so obviously it's more fun for me."

"Really? You look a bit tense." Ok she didn't really but we're all allowed a bitchy moment. "A bit drawn."

She stared at herself in the mirror. Looking for validation. "Really?"

"Just a little. Maybe you're worried about something. And maybe you should be," I tossed over my shoulder as I left the ladies room. OK so that wasn't my finest moment, but everyone is, as I say allowed, one bitchy comment and that woman was really getting on my nerves. It was like I had an itch and I simply had to scratch it. Maybe she really was worried she wouldn't get Teddy back. The reality was I was more worried she would.

Back out in the function center the crowd was mercifully starting to thin.

Jane came up to say good-bye to Joyce and Bob and me.

"He's just on his final interview, and he'll be done. It's great. He's done a host of interviews and he'll get some great press. Every mum will be getting one of these books, come Mother's Day. Well I hope I see you before Teddy goes, Bob and Joyce."

"If he goes Jane, it's not in the bag yet." Bob, ever practical.

"I have a good feeling." Jane didn't look like a woman with psychic abilities. She was a sensible looking woman with a black bob and black flat shoes. She was wearing well-cut black pants, about 8 strings of jade beads and a white shirt. She looked lovely, but she did not look psychic. "Well fingers crossed anyway. I have to get home and relieve the sitter, Glen's on the night shift. See you."

"Glen's a doctor." It was quite handy having Joyce about she was a font of knowledge. "But poor Jane, she's had such a tough time."

"Oh."

"Yes, Glen, slipped in the shower about four years ago, she was pregnant at the time. Anyway it was a freak accident, but he ended up in a wheelchair. He's a quadriplegic or paraplegic. Which one is it Bob? I always get those two confused?"

"Para, I believe, dear."

"Gosh, that's terrible."

"Yes, it was quite dreadful. Teddy was with her when she had the baby, because Glen was immobile and she went into labour at work."

"Oh, my goodness."

"Yes, she was lucky to have Teddy. He's the baby's godfather of course. Little Nick is he cutest thing ever."

"I bet he is!"

"Teddy was a big help to them. He helped find a nurse and he got all the people from the show in and they modified the house with ramps and things so it was accessible. Glen's back at work now, but it's a limited capacity thing, unfortunately."

I tried to wrap my mind around all that. Poor Jane. And Teddy helping her so much. Being at a birth, that's a big thing. And now being married to a paraplegic, I didn't know much about that but I did know it was almost a full-time job helping someone manage in that condition, at least initially, while they learnt to adjust. Then again I suppose she needed to work to support them. What an amazing woman she must be. It was all quite humbling really.

"Louisa was very jealous of all the time it took away from her, silly girl. That was one of the issues."

"Joyce!" Bob's voice was stern and reprimanding.

"Sorry, mustn't gossip. Anyway, I can't believe Teddy didn't tell you. He's a bit modest, our Ted."

Modest, distracted, sweet, generous, inconsistent and very confusing, were my impressions of "our Ted."

Teddy came over and it was time to go. He pulled me aside as Joyce and Bob headed out front.

"Please, come back. I feel like I haven't spoken to you, or seen you all day."

"Yeah, I know the feeling."

"I'm sorry, it's been so nuts. I wanted you to see my life, to get to know me better."

"Yeah, I know and I learnt a ton about your job, which by the way I think you're great at, and the launch was fun too but..."

"But?"

"But, it's been a long day and it's time to go home. And really you should spend some time with your folks too."

Teddy hailed me a cab after I'd said good-bye to his parents.

"Darling, it was lovely to meet you."

"Yes, a pleasure Allegra. We'll see you soon."

Teddy planted a kiss on my forehead as he planted me in the cab.

"I will see you tomorrow. I'll call you first up, OK?"

"OK. Congrats again on the book. It's an amazing achievement."

"Thanks. And thanks for being there for me. It meant everything." He kissed me this time hard on the lips.

The door closed and I was travelling back across the Harbour Bridge as the lights twinkled in buildings all around the harbour foreshore.

It was a strange feeling. I'd spent the day with Teddy and seen into his world. I should have been thrilled that he wanted me there. I should have been ecstatic he wanted me to meet his parents.

So how come I really felt in my heart that I really didn't belong in his world?

And why did I feel like I didn't belong?

It certainly wasn't because anyone had been unkind or unwelcoming, obviously aside from Louisa. It was just that his world didn't feel like a good fit for me.

His world felt like a pair of very high sparkly stilettos. Glamorous, gorgeous and uncomfortable. My world was like a nice pair of summer slides. Bright, easy and functional.

Sitting there in that taxi, with the driver listening to inane talk-back radio, it occurred to me once and for all that I really did want to fit into Teddy's life. I was really starting to feel just like the rest of the nation: that I was just a little bit in love with Teddy Green.

Chapter Sixteen

I opened up the shop on Wednesday morning and my sister Deb came racing in just after 10am in her usual chaotic way. She was there to work but there really wasn't too much to do. Lucie had held the fort well the day before and apparently we'd been really busy. That was always nice news to come back to. I did have some paper-work piling up out back that needed doing, but frankly that wasn't the day for it. Of course no one is ever in the mood to do tax, but some days are more conducive than others.

Deb was dying to catch up on the gossip on my weekend date as well as the details of the day before on set. Personally I was feeling a bit luke-warm about the whole thing by then. That was a real shame, because Deb was such an enthusiast and such a romantic and she really deserved the feel-good date story.

And I honestly did do my best to talk it up. That wasn't too hard when it came to the date because it really had been good, aside from the pond incident, which even Deb was horrified by.

The day before with the show and the book launch sounded flat, I was sure, because that was how I felt about it and I am simply not a very good actress. Sadly, I lack my mother's capacity for exaggeration. Deb still seemed quite impressed by it all and thought I was just being negative. I think in her life or barbeques, tuck shop, dance lessons and motherhood anything out of the ordinary was exciting, no matter how dull the reality for the participant.

Deb was just launching into a heart-felt lecture on the course of true love and how it never runs smooth. "Allegra, it is a great mystery to me how anyone with Johno Johnson for a father can be as big a pessimist as you are."

Just then the shop door tinkled its bell and in walked the man himself, Johno. He was carrying a tray of coffees for us and wearing his usual jolly grin.

"Who is a pessimist? I hope not one of my girls!" His big sunny presence lit up the room.

A funny thing about Johno and I was that whenever he wasn't in the room with me I had a kind of ache to know he was near. And as the man lived in Byron Bay more than an eight-hour drive away, that ache was pretty constant. I am fairly certain it was due to the way he was so unceremoniously ripped away from me and out of my life as a child.

I ached for my mother because of what she was not. With Johno, I ached for all that he was. All love and good will.

He engulfed me in a bear hug.

"You didn't know your dear old dad was coming to town did you Ally?"

"Nope."

"Last minute thing. I had some business stuff and some other things on so I thought. "Why not come and see my non-Byron girls?""

"Will you be seeing all three?" I asked thinking about Rebecca.

"Well, darlin', I'll try." He sipped his cappuccino, which knowing him was a soy decaf. "So what are we feeling pessimistic about?"

"Allegra is being pessimistic about her new boyfriend but I think she's being ridiculous!" Well tell it like you see it Deb.

"Ally I don't know a thing about the fellow so you had better give me the full story."

Explaining things to Johno was like explaining it to one of the girls, or Justin, he sat and listened and nodded. Interjecting with the odd "So then what" or an "Oh really?" and a "what you're saying then is". He was a very blokey male with some excellent new-age mirroring technique going on.

In the end he agreed with Deb that I was worrying over nothing.

"Allegra, what are you worried about? It sounds like he likes you to me. You're just projecting your anxiety onto him. I mean the man was launching a book and schmoozing the media, what did you expect he'd be doing all night, standing right next to you?"

"I suppose not."

"Just roll with it. I know that's not entirely in your nature, but give it a whirl."

"I can try." I tried to be stoic.

"That's my girl. Remember what your grandmother Nancy, always said – Good things come to those who wait."

I supposed he was right. It wasn't as if Teddy had done anything wrong. I mean it was always going to be a pretty weird event for me with all those TV types, plus meeting the parents.

I was starting to feel a bit better about the prospect of Teddy Green and me.

Johno decided he'd come back at 1pm and we'd shut up shop and go out to lunch. I never shut the shop during regular hours but it wasn't as if the whole enterprise would crumble if it was closed for an hour.

"We'll have a drink, we'll relax and I can fill you in on all the gossip from home."

The morning was pretty steady and I did sneak out the back and shuffle some papers around so I didn't feel so guilty.

I made a few calls about Lisa's hen's day planned for the upcoming Saturday including one to the bride herself, during school recess.

"Hey Lisa, quick call. Is your mum in or out for Saturday? I have to finalise the numbers."

"She's out."

"Ok, probably for the best."

"Is Teddy in or out for the wedding? Mum is finalising numbers? And she is getting a little crazy."

"Give me till tonight."

"OK, gotta go."

Just before we were due to go to lunch Deb called out to me from the front of the store.

"Ally, can you come up here?"

I meandered through the store and there at the front counter looking dazzling in a blue shirt was Teddy. He was holding my bag from the day before in one hand and a big pot of lavender with a gorgeous purple ribbon around it in the other.

"Hey, Ally."

"Hey, Teddy, did you meet my sister Deb?"

"Uhmm yes we met, though she didn't say she was your sister. Cool." He grinned at Deb, handed me the flowers and kissed me hard on the mouth in one fluid movement.

"Thanks, they're beautiful, but you didn't need to do that."

"No, but I wanted to."

The thing about having Teddy in the room was that it reminded me how much I really liked him. Of course there was the extreme cuteness but he also had this lovely, calm aura.

"Thanks again. Not working today?" I asked.

"No, I get the day off for good behavior. So I spent the morning with my folks before they headed back to Bathurst."

"Your parents were lovely, I thought."

"They thought you were lovely too." Charmer.

"Of course they did." Deb was leaning over the counter and just couldn't help but join in. "She is lovely."

"Deb is the protective sister in the family." The doorbell tinkled and in walked Johno. "And here is my way less protective father."

Teddy turned to be confronted by the big bear of a man that is Johno. He was wearing a bizarre kaftan-style top over cheesecloth pants. What's even more bizarre is that when he was in earlier I hadn't noticed his clothes. Funny how I was now seeing him as if through new eyes. And being Johno, he was also wearing an enormous grin.

"Well, well, well Teddy, nice to meet you." And then poor Teddy was engulfed in an enormous Johno hug. He came out looking remarkably unperturbed.

"It's nice to meet you too."

"The girls and I were about to head out for some lunch. Do you want to come with us?"

"Sure. Great." OK the whole meet the family thing seemed so easy for Teddy, why had it been so stressful for me?

"Well Ally, let's shut up shop!

We found ourselves at the pub of Johno's choice - the Arms. It was his old hang from his pre-Moonbeam days and he still knew plenty of semi-retired blokes like himself who hung out there. Walking into the bar was pretty much like walking into Johno's 60th birthday party a few weeks earlier, back on that fateful day when I'd first met Teddy.

Johno's concession to us was to have lunch at the groovy new restaurant on the roof, but only after we all had a drink in the main bar.

"I'll get the first round," Teddy offered magnanimously.

"Don't be ridiculous, mate. You're buying the lunch." We must have all paled. "Just joking. Ally's buying the lunch mate, so I'll get the drinks." I knew he wasn't joking about that part, not that I cared.

The public bar was as it had always been – swirly RSL carpet, high tables with stools, and tables built along the window to take in the killer view. And of course there was the unmistakable stench of stale beer synonymous with pubs the world over. Johno got the drinks while we found a table. I was regretting having worn this shortish flippy skirt as I perched on the barstool. Too much leg was showing and Teddy wasn't the only one looking. There is something consistently disturbing about your father's friend leering at your legs, and that holds true whether you are fifteen or twenty-eight.

Johno was carrying two beers and two champagnes on a traditional chrome pub-style tray. He needed a free hand to wave at people he knew so that was, I'm sure, why he hadn't gone the traditional bouquet of glasses that men run from the bar to the table with, spilling as they go.

"I think your Dad has the makings of a great celebrity Deb," Teddy noted as Dad sauntered back nodding and waving to old mates.

"He's long been infamous in these parts. That's enough of an ego trip for him."

"Who's on an ego trip?"

"You are Dad." Deb was not one to back away.

"I'm not ashamed of that. I've done a lot of work on myself in the last 20 years. I've worked hard on my Id."

"Bloody Freudian hippy mumbo jumbo, Dad. You always had an enormous ego; you didn't need a workshop to help you with that." She was laughing as she paid him out.

"True enough. But now I don't have to feel guilty about it." He cleared his throat and raised his glass, "Right let's toast. To family and to new friends." How can you argue with that? So we all toasted.

"So, Teddy, have you heard about that new job yet?"

"No, sir, I haven't, should be any day now."

"Teddy I think we'll get along great if you just don't call me sir. It makes me feel ancient."

"OK." Big gulp of beer.

"So, Teddy where will you live if you just up and go to LA?"

That was a good question. I hadn't even thought to ask that. Deb was very practical. I think she got that from her mother. Not having a practical mother at all I guess I had nowhere to get such skills from.

"Well they have an apartment lined up for me for six months in Hollywood. It's somewhere pretty close to the studio I think."

"Well mate I hope you get it, but just remember money isn't everything. Oh it's very helpful but it isn't everything, is it Ally?"

"Uhm no Dad, I'm sure Teddy knows that."

"Oh, I'm sure but you know you have to keep it in mind when making any big deal. You don't get that money for nothing. I learnt that in real estate, long ago."

"Still work in Real Estate, Johno?" Nice subject change.

"Well, I'm more in property management, like Ally, I guess."

"Dad, I'm not IN property management, I run a bookshop!" I was really hoping he'd shut up. I hated talking about money and especially in front of Deb, who basically had none. And I really didn't want to discuss my financial situation with Teddy at length either.

"Darlin' you run a bookshop and you manage a host of properties. And really the bookshop is just a hobby as far as I am concerned."

OK that made me mad. "Look Johno, it's not a hobby as far as I'm concerned. It's my life, OK."

"All I'm saying darlin' is that it may be where you spend your time but it's not your primary source of income."

"But Johno weren't you the one just saying money isn't everything?" asked Teddy. Good point. OK, maybe I really did love Teddy. I did at that moment anyway...

Thank heavens Johno let it go when one of his cronies came over to chat with him.

"He's very verbose today isn't he?" chipped in Deb who'd been rather quiet.

"Yep Deb, he sure is. I think he's trying to be fatherly."

"I think he's easier to handle when he's stoned, quite frankly," Deb suggested as she sipped her wine.

"Is that common?" Teddy looked a bit surprised. I guess Mr Green Senior wasn't the kind of Dad who had a regular joint after dinner.

"Oh, yeah, though he's usually pretty straight down here, just up in Byron he relaxes more."

I leaned in to Teddy as Johno was turning back, "And just think, this is my responsible parent." It boggled the mind really.

Lunch itself was much smoother. Teddy got chatty and Johno mellowed out after a few beers.

The food was lovely and the view out over Manly beach was superb.

As Johno had planned lunch was indeed on me.

"Well Deb, we'd better get back to work."

"So, Ally, do you want me to drive to Birchgrove to get your car?"

"You'd have to hang around a while."

"Just go Ally, I'll man the fort," offered Deb.

"But I was off yesterday."

"Live a little sweetie. I promise not to clean out the till."

So it was decided I would go with Teddy back to Balmain and get the van.

First we went upstairs, I wanted to change into a more comfy skirt at least and it was hot so I wanted to put my hair up…the old Kombi has no air-conditioning so you need to dress light for hot days.

He wandered around the living room while I changed. He was sitting on the couch with his elbows resting on his knees when I returned.

"Listen baby," he looked so earnest as I came down the hall. "Are we OK? I feel as if somehow something shifted last night."

I sat beside him. "No, well…maybe… it was just a weird day for me. It was like this whole other world, and I'm not too sure I fit into that world. That's all."

"Of course you fit. It's just one of those worlds where no one feels like they fit."

"You do."

"No! I may *look* like I fit but I don't always *feel* like I fit. There is a lot of expectation that I do certain things and I try to meet my obligations but often it feels kind of surreal."

"Well I'm just not sure it's a world I feel comfortable in, that's all."

"Give it a chance. And after all I'm more than just my job. What's important is how we fit together. And I bet that is great." I was sure there was some innuendo intended by the somewhat lecherous look on his face but I decided to ignore it.

"True, but your job is kind of looming large just now...what with the maybe-move and all."

"Yeah. It is. I'm hoping to hear today or tomorrow about LA. The suspense is starting to get to me."

"Me too! Especially as I really want you to get it, and of course I also selfishly don't."

"That's not selfish. I'm just glad to hear you want me around." He nudged me.

"Of course I do." I nudged him back. "Shall we go get my car?"

"OK, but even though I know this wasn't really a fight but do you think we could kiss and make up anyway? I've been missing you these past few days." Well who would say no to that?

Chapter Seventeen

"So do you want to come to my house or shall I come to yours?" Teddy was asking as I was about to climb out of the ute having already checked the street for any sign of stray dogs. There was often one lurking about in the inner city suburbs, just waiting to pounce on me, I had found.

"Very presumptuous, Mr Green."

"I just want to be with you."

"OK, come to my place. I'll make you dinner. Justin is in WA for a week so that works. Give me till six."

"See you then."

I started to walk away and then I waved him down as he headed past me up the road.

He hit the button and rolled down the passenger side window.

"What did you forget?"

"I forgot to ask you something."

"What?"

"I don't suppose you'd like to come to Lisa's wedding with me next weekend?"

His adorable face lit up in a grin. "I thought you'd never ask!"

"So that would be a yes?"

"A definite yes."

When I got in the van I sat there and thought.

Well, Allegra, this is it. There is a limit to how often you can send Australia's sexiest man home without satisfaction. Not, that I imagined, would be any hardship involved there, but still I didn't want to be feeling foolish after the fact.

After I had stopped by the fish markets to get some oysters for dinner, I called Justin. Of course his dad answered because it was 2pm on the other side of the country. I could tell he'd obviously had a long lunch with plenty of home-grown wine. Good for him.

"Hey Ally, how are you? Juz, who is out, by the way, tells me you have a new boyfriend. Good for you."

"Well I don't know if he's really my boyfriend…"

"Listen, take some advice from an old fool, give love a chance. Let people in."

"Has Justin been talking…?" I should have known it was the wine that was talking.

"Sweetie, you are like one of my own I look back now and wish I had done better by you."

"What could you have done? My mother…"

"Well, Ally, I don't know exactly what I should have done but the point is someone should have done something and no one did. It takes a village."

"I think there's a book…"

"Thanks for the advice. I'll try to follow it."

"OK sweetie. I'll tell Justin to call you."

"Tomorrow Ok, not at 3am tonight, as is his custom."

"Tomorrow it is. I won't even tell him you called until then."

Teddy arrived promptly at 6pm. He looked gorgeous in a crisp white shirt and jeans. And he had that lemony smell again.

"Hey, baby!" He pulled me into a warm embrace for a hello kiss. Well it was warm apart from the cold bottle of champagne being held against my back.

"Hey you! Come on in."

I had tidied up the apartment so that, unlike his first visit, there were no piles of newspapers or baskets of laundry cluttering the living room. Of course there were still books wherever you looked, but that's how I like my home. Late afternoon summer sun streamed in and I thought all in all it looked rather nice.

The flowers he'd given me earlier in the day shared the center of the coffee table with a plate of Turkish bread, some tarramasalata and a bowl of spicy olives. I wandered into the kitchen to get some champagne glasses.

I had a strange feeling inside and stopped to ponder it. I had a beautiful home and a damn cute boyfriend. The feeling I was experiencing was quite unmistakable. It was that rare and exquisite feeling known as happiness.

"So what shall we toast?" I asked as I carried the glasses into the living room.

"Well…I have some news…" and right then that happy feeling vanished. Ah well, I'd had my moment.

"You got the job!" Fake joy sprung from my mouth.

"I got the job. I leave Sunday week." Real joy sprung from Teddy.

Hold it together, Allegra. Don't pass out. You knew it was coming. This is what he wants. This is who he is. You knew it was happening, now look happy for him, and blink back the tears.

"Wow! Well that is cause for celebration. Open those bubbles. Quick let's toast." He did so and filled our glasses with what I then noticed was vintage Moet. "To your success!"

We sipped and he leant in and gave me a very long, slow champagney kiss. And all I could think was how do I get myself out of this situation.

"So you got the call. Tell me all."

Some guy called Merv phoned earlier and gave him the news. It had been down to him and some Pommy fellow but they liked the Australian angle, apparently Australia was more fashion forward than the UK for American TV. Who knew? Teddy had spent the afternoon calling his folks and Jane setting things in motion.

"What happens to the show here?"

He swallowed his bread and dip before answering." This is great dip."

"Thanks I made it."

"You should be a chef. You're a brilliant cook"

"Maybe. About the show?"

"Oh yeah, my contract is currently under renegotiation anyway...so I'm out. They'll keep me under a different agreement. I'll do a couple of specials and celebrity things a year. Like the Christmas carols, you know that sort of stuff."

"Do you sing?"

"No. I usually host them." He smiled at me in that amused way he reserved for the times when I showed my overwhelming ignorance for all things celebrity and TV related.

"So everything is all taken care of?" Except me.

"Pretty much. I'm going to leave my place empty for now since I'm renting a furnished place in LA first up, and I'll be back and forth a bit to start I think."

So that was it. It was all settled. Teddy was leaving and that was that.

"I'll just go check the dinner." I had to get out of there. I didn't want to say anything pathetic or desperate or clingy. I certainly didn't want to say anything to rain on his parade. That pretty much eliminated all the thoughts that were into my head at that time.

In the kitchen I stood staring at the oven. Then I opened and shut it so that it would sound like I was doing something useful, when really I wasn't.

How had I gotten myself into this mess?

I turned around to see Teddy leaning on the doorframe holding his champagne.

"Ally, are you OK?"

"Sure. Why do you ask?"

"Because you're crying."

"No I'm not!" But when I reached my hand up my face was wet. So I figured he was right. "Oh sorry, must be the onion." Nice recovery, I thought. Good to see I could think on my feet

"What onion?" He was looking around trying to spot a half-chopped onion I guess. Of course there wasn't one.

"Look it's a kitchen, of course there is onion." Faking again. He walked across the kitchen and enfolded me in his arms. And I very embarrassingly started to sob.

"Must be a whole bag of onions in here huh?" His voice was all gooey. "Listen baby…"

"Ok, I'm not up for a listen baby conversation just now Teddy."

"Not even listen baby, let's go sit down and I'll pour you another champagne?"

"OK that I can probably handle. I'll just bring out the oysters."

"Oh I love oysters! Very romantic."

"I have to tell you your chances for romance were a whole lot better an hour ago."

"I figured that." Smart guy. "I did consider not telling you till later, but I figured that was a bit low."

"You think?" I shook my head at him as I put the oysters out.

"Just a bit." He handed me the topped up champagne and I basically inhaled it.

"OK, I feel a little better now. Look I really am happy for you, Teddy. I'm just not good at good-byes."

"Who said anything about goodbye?"

"Excuse me, but you are about to move to LA! It seems somewhat inevitable to me. Can I offer you an oyster? There are three toppings: natural, vodka and caviar and a tomato and basil style salsa."

He just sat there shaking his head at me. Then he stood up took the oyster plate and put it down on the table. He held me firmly by the shoulders and looked into my eyes.

"Allegra, listen to me very carefully, the oysters look amazing but let's just wait on them a minute. Nobody is saying goodbye to anybody. I really, really like you. I may even be in love with you so I don't think this is the time for goodbyes. OK? I want to be with you. Got it?"

"Got it! But…" Did he just say he was in love with me?

"What's with the but?" He paused,"Sheesh, now I'm even doing the 'but' thing!"

"The but is…but you're moving…and I just figure it's easier to sort of break up now and…"

"I don't know why you keep thinking I want to dump you all the time! It's very annoying." He turned away, sipped his champagne and ran his hand through his hair in what looked like quiet desperation. "Ally, can I ask you a personal question?"

"Sure, I guess."

"Why did you break up with your last boyfriend?"

"Do I have to answer that?"

"I'd like it if you would. Because I'm kind of tired of trying to make up for his behavior, whoever he was, when I don't even know what he did. It can't have been that bad"

"If you really want to know, I'll tell you." I plopped down on the couch and sighed. Teddy was looking at me with such concern. I took a large gulp of my drink. "OK, my last boyfriend slept with my mother."

"Are you serious?" He looked like I had punched him. It was an actual physical reaction. Then he landed beside me on the couch.

"Yeah, he slept with my mother. I never saw it coming. It was somewhat devastating at the time."

"I'll bet." He was very quiet.

"Anyway, needless to say I have some trust issues."

"Understandable."

"And let's just say I already had some trust issues before that."

"Why?"

"You really do not want to know."

"Maybe I do."

"I doubt it."

"I don't think you give me enough credit."

"I just told you I had trust issues, Teddy."

"OK, good point."

We just sat there sipping our champagne for a while.

"Do you have anything to say Teddy?"

"I'm looking for the right words. Frankly, I do better with a script." He ran his hand through his hair again.

"I'm sure we all would. It's a pity life is not like that!"

"Look, Ally, I'm floored about the whole thing. Firstly I can't even fathom why anyone who could be with you would choose to blow it by being with Moonbeam. That is so beyond my ability to comprehend. I seriously don't know what to do with that."

"Imagine how I feel!" I was back on the champagne.

"And then I can only guess at the rest. But I've met Moonbeam and Johno so I have inkling."

"Let's just say while your parents were taking you on picnics, we were moving communes. And that was the good times while Johno was still with us."

"Do you blame him?"

"No, Johno was a victim too. But we were apart a long time and it is hard for him to live up to my fantasy dad."

"He has fallen a little short, huh?"

"Of course."

"So you have kind of always been on your own."

"And lonely." That must be the wine.

"Yeah, so I understand that you expect everyone to leave you and I don't know how to counter that." He kissed my forehead.

"Look, Teddy, you've known me three weeks and I don't expect you to change my past, but I just have to be smart about my future."

"Of course you do". He was holding my hand and moving his fingers lightly over mine. He picked it up and started kissing the fingertips. "You have to be smart."

"And the smart thing is for me to accept you're leaving."

"Maybe I am leaving…but I am not leaving YOU, there is a difference. And I'm going to be the most important part of your future, baby, I can promise you that. You only have two decisions to make right now." He was kissing my neck slowly just beneath my left ear.

"What are they?" I was finding it a bit hard to concentrate what with the crying, the champagne and the emotional sharing all whizzing about in my brain. And now added to that was the fantastic kissing which had moved around to my mouth.

He pulled back and looked dreamily at me.

"First you have to decide whether you trust me or not and second whether you want me to make you very happy at this very moment."

Oh such easy decisions. "And, baby, they're not necessarily mutually exclusive." More kissing.

Look I'm not a nun and I'm not a saint and I am pretty sure you need to be Catholic to be either, and that's another thing I'm not. I had the words of my friends and Justin's dad whizzing in my brain and I thought well, this is it.

This amazing guy is here right now and if he debunks to the northern hemisphere next week will I look back and think, you had your chance and you blew it or will I think good thing he left and you didn't enjoy yourself while you had a shot. That seemed pathetic even by my standards.

So naturally I leant towards fantastic if temporary satisfaction.

And while I am not one to kiss and tell I must tell you that I was one hundred percent correct in my decision for that moment. And I would make it the same way again, which frankly isn't something I often think. And I was also correct in my belief that anyone who kisses as well as Teddy…well, you know they have to have skills in other areas.

And afterwards, as we were propped up amongst the many pillows, on my very girly bed, eating the cold and somewhat burnt chicken we had forgotten in the oven, I again felt that rare and wondrous feeling known as happiness.

"Well, baby, I have to say that was worth waiting for."

"Me or the chicken?"

"Both!"

"Hmm. Well I still haven't decided if I trust you for the longer term, but you were right about the moment, at least."

"I aim to please."

"Good to know."

"Here is what I know, Ally. I think you're amazing! I love being near you. I can't wait to talk to you, to see you, to touch you and to me that must mean something."

"We call that lust, Teddy."

"You think?" he said while doing things I'm not about to tell you about.

"Definitely!"

"I think you're wrong. I know lust. I'm a lusty bloke."

"You sound like a pirate!"

"Well, I know lust and this is more than that. I don't usually do lunch with the father for lust."

"Good point. What about dinner with the gay friend?"

"Maybe, but not the gay friend *and* the psycho mother."

"Fair enough."

"Look, all I'm saying Ally, is that this is more than that. I know it in my heart. I wish you did too."

"Maybe your heart is a more reliable guide."

"This time I think it is."

I didn't really get much sleep that night.

We decided to decamp to my large old-fashioned-claw-footed bath. We had some more champagne and just kind of chit chatted about things.

And Teddy gave me the most mind blowing foot rub I've ever had. I guess there is something to be said for rugged manly hands that are used to hard work. My own hands tend to cramp mid-foot rub, but that was not a problem for Mr. Green. It was so good it was almost orgasmic, though I am sure that had something to do with my frame of mind.

"Wow, I am going to have to pay you back big-time for that."

"I am sure we can find a way."

"You think?"

There really is something rather wonderful about snuggling up with someone after the fact. Well, that is if you really like the person and are not swamped by regret or embarrassment, neither of which appeared to afflict either of us that night.

CHAPTER EIGHTEEN

I was woken at 4am by Teddy gently kissing me goodbye.

"Baby, I have to go to Broken Hill today. My flight is at 6.30am. We're filming a drought resistant garden show, it's at a women's shelter. It's my last show."

"Oh, OK. When are you back?"

"Saturday. Will I see you then?"

"I have Lisa's hen's day. It's an all day thing."

"Well, I have a work dinner Saturday night so can we meet Sunday?"

"Sure."

"Listen, I want you to think about something..."I sat up and leaned dozily against the bed-head.

"Sure."

"Think about coming to LA with me."

"Teddy! I don't think..."

"Look, just think about it, OK?" He kissed me as he flew out the door. I heard the apartment door slam.

And he was gone. And I was lying there wide awake wondering what in hell I was doing.

It shouldn't have been a shock to me. The signs had been there. Lisa had asked me what I would say if he asked me to go, Jane had hinted, but still I had just thought that they were nuts. No one asks someone to move to another continent with them after three weeks of dating, surely?

It was just pillow talk I figured. Unnecessary. He could have just snuck out.

Or sent flowers. Even though I was already awash with flowers.

Or said "Let's see what happens."

I got up and made a cup of tea. I got back into bed and drank it very, very slowly.

***

Around 6am I got up and went for a long gentle run along the beach. I love watching the sun pop up over the ocean and seeing the beach come alive.

People emerge from apartments to surf, fish, run and stroll along the beach. They head out for early cups of coffee or breakfast before work. Groups of young surfers pile out of vans then pull on their wetsuits and hit the waves. Japanese backpackers with streaked orange hair sit on the seawall and smoke.

And then all of a sudden it's daytime and the place is buzzing with families carrying beach toys, towels and buckets down to the waters edge. They're out to make the most of the day before the beach is too hot to enjoy.

By the time I got back home and opened the shop my head was a little clearer. It was my day in there alone and I was grateful. After what seemed like weeks of talking about myself to my friends and family, it was nice to just stack books and serve customers and enjoy the quiet. I even got some of that nasty tax done.

The day seemed normal, like my old pre-Teddy life. Cherie in the beautician's was flat out so I dropped her in a coffee from the café when I got mine, and as was tradition I flirted a little with George from the coffee shop when I collected my take-away salad at lunchtime.

Bang on closing time I shut up shop and headed upstairs to do my laundry and clean up the dishes from the night before. I felt firmly planted back in my life, where I belonged. If I tried hard enough, every so often I could even forget about Teddy.

It wasn't that I wasn't mad about him. It was just that everything was going so fast and I wasn't quite sure I was ready for what he thought he was ready for, and come to think of it, I wasn't so sure he was ready for it either.

By 7pm I was perched in my favourite wing chair thinking about my situation.

The only reason I was here at all was because of my grandmother Nancy. I can't even imagine where I would have been had I not ended up with her when my mother abandoned me to hit the Asian the hippy trail about 20 years after most of the hippies left.

What can I tell you about my grandmother, Nancy? She was a character.

She married my grandfather quite late and I think she'd had a rather colourful time prior to that. After all, my mother got her wild spirit from somewhere and it wasn't my grandfather. I know my great-grandmother had lamented the fact that Nancy would never settle down and everyone thought Percy, my grandfather, an unlikely choice.

He was a gentle, introverted man. He loved football, cricket and a beer with the lads. Apart from his time in the army, he never lived anywhere but Manly and said upon his return, "I'm never living anywhere else in my entire bloody life."

It was one of the few blanket statements he ever made. He was like that, very careful with his words, so when he said something you knew he really meant it.

My grandmother was a fiery redhead with long legs and a streak of individuality. She came from an affluent family who did not approve of Percy and, Nancy being Nancy she didn't give a toss.

Whatever it was that attracted them to each other saw them through fifty years and a lot of heartache, so it was something, for sure.

They tried for a long time to have kids and then gave up.

My grandmother started her second hand shop and became a well-known figure around the traps in Manly. So it was a huge but welcome shock when my mother Sophia was born when Nancy was well in her forties.

In the meantime my grandparents just kept buying bits of property up all over the area; a flat here, a house there, a shop there. My grandfather was a builder and would hear that people were moving on they'd buy them out. No one knew the extent of his or her holdings until my grandmother passed.

"We just wanted to make sure your mother always had enough, for all the good it did us."

My grandmother managed their properties and holdings from the back of the bookshop in between long lunches, world cruises and ladies poker games.

She baked all her own cakes, gave generously to the poor and provided free or subsidised housing to friends who hadn't faired so well.

She never wore skirts, only trousers.

"If it's good enough for Katherine Hepburn, then it's good enough for me."

And old Nancy could drink like a fish. She began on the gin and tonics at 6pm on the dot or 'cocktail hour' as she referred to it. She moved her drinking through many hours before the evening was over but only the first hour was given a name.

So if you had to ask her for anything about 7pm was the ideal time. Too early and she might refuse you and too late and she might not remember.

She always wore Chanel No 5, and red lipstick.

My grandmother swam in the small ocean pool outside their block of flats, every morning year round, until the last year of her life.

"Clears your head," she'd say.

She had no time for retirement or those who espoused it. She believed that was the beginning of the end. She never let Grandpa retire and she certainly never did either. The poor man was doing odd jobs until his late 70s.

"Why shouldn't he? He can still hammer a nail for God's sake."

When I came to live with my grandmother, I was sixteen and she was in her mid-seventies.

At first I thought she didn't like me or want me around, but I came to understand that the only thing worse for my grandmother than having a grandchild out there, whom you had never met, was the fear of meeting her and losing her again.

Until the day I moved in I had never met my grandmother.

When my mother decided that she needed to travel through Asia, along the hippy trail. I'm not sure how long the idea had been brewing or what possessed her to execute it at that precise moment but just after I turned sixteen we drove from where we were in Queensland to Byron Bay where my Dad was living. Her need to up and move on in the middle of the night was no longer surprising to me.

At the crack of a summer dawn she bundled me out of the car and we knocked together on someone's front door. The man who opened the door was my Dad, Johno.

I'm not sure who was more shocked, Johno or me, as we hadn't seen each other in seven years.

My mother turned to him and said, "I'm going to India. She's your problem now."

And to me she said, "I've done my best Allegra, but now I need to put myself first". As if she had been the world's most selfless parent.

She took herself back to the car and drove off. I stood there speechless. On the one hand here was my father...on the other there went my mother.

A month later for a host of reasons not the least of which was newly born twin siblings in ICU and Johno's new wife, who is a fantastic lady but who at that moment was in no position to take on a teenager, I found myself again on someone's doorstep and that someone was my grandmother, Nancy.

She had always known I existed because of my Dad, but she'd never met me and, had we passed each other in the street the day before, we would not have known each other.

She decided that rather than my living with her and Percy, I should live above the bookshop. She was there all day and thought it would enable her to keep an eye on me but give us both some independence.

I used to have dinner with them most nights anyway so it all worked out.

"We know you're used to a lot of space, Allegra, and we don't want to overwhelm you".

It seemed a little odd to me at first, and my friends simply could not believe

I had my own apartment, but I can see now it was genius. I wasn't used to being part of a family and neither was she.

We had a ball decorating the place and then, at least, I had my own permanent home, something that had eluded me until that point.

I suppose it was a rather strange set up but it lasted through Percy's death and then her own four years ago.

I felt so blessed to have been welcomed into her world and then entrusted with it.

Sitting there that night I really could not imagine giving up the only home I'd ever had for some guy, who though thoroughly spectacular, I had only known for under a month.

But then the phone rang…and it was him. "Hey baby…" and I thought… well, maybe.

CHAPTER NINETEEN

I woke up all raring to go for Lisa's hen's day. Actually I woke up when I heard Justin letting himself in the front door. He was fresh from the Perth red-eye and from visiting his dad.

I met Justin in the kitchen where we convened for tea, toast and a Teddy update. What I actually got a colourful blow-by-blow description of his clubbing and winery experiences in Perth.

Why is it that some people can make the most mundane things seem hilarious? During his week in Perth, Justin had an encounter with a crazed nun on a bus, taken a gay Swedish football team on a pub crawl and played doting uncle to his sister's kids. He was a maniac!

"So, Ally, ready for an exciting hen's day my little chick?"

"Ready as I'll ever be."

We were starting the day with a pampering cruise. One of the things that give me the irits about hen's days and the like is that you always end up paying a fortune to do something that you very possibly don't even want to do. So, to make sure there were no whining and reluctant participants I had decided to just pay for everyone. Aside from Caroline, no one else knew who was paying, so I didn't look like a show-off or have to be thanked.

We were all meeting at the wharf at ten, so I went and got the bride, who had no idea what her day had in store on the way.

"Come on little bride! Let's go have some fun."

There were twenty of us in all. Lisa's three sisters-in-law and Mike's sister and cousin, a few of Lisa's cousins, some of Lisa's colleagues from FernHill , a few other friends and her future mother-in-law.

The whole day was both amazing and hilarious. I could see why these cruises were the thing for hen's days and girl's days out because everything was done for you. The cruise started with champagne and canapés and everyone had facials, massages and manicures. There was even a clairvoyant on board for the eager, which after several hours of champagne and cruising was just about everyone. Even I had to have a turn so as I didn't look like a party pooper.

I don't hold much stock in clairvoyants because Moonbeam has posed as one from to time to time to make money and given her ability to see what will happen in an hour is worse than most people's she had kind of sucked all credibility out of all things mystical for me. On the other hand Johno swears he knows people who really can see your future and your past lives and read your aura. I am not saying it is good to be a skeptic, just that I am one.

"Come, my child; let's see what the future holds."

"Ok, then." What did I have to lose?

"I see a man with lovely eyes."

"That could be my father."

"No this is a lover." Blush. "A new lover, I think."

And I see a journey." OK she was sucking me in.

"Really?"

"Yes. And I see books, do you work with books?"

"Yes"

"Well now this man with the eyes...I see trouble close by. But then I see happiness, maybe."

"Maybe?" That was not very uplifting.

"And I see something else. There was a fork in the road. Yes a fork...and the paths split…" That is true for all people I thought. Everyone has forks. Everyone has Robert Frost road not taken moments. "I think it was a career or a job choice."

"Yes."

"There was a creative choice and a sensible choice. You chose the sensible choice." There was a safe chance of that, I mean everyone makes the sensible choice sometimes don't they? "Well I see you getting another chance at the creative choice. Did you think about becoming a designer?"

Indeed I did. "Uhm yes."

"Well, my dear, I think you are about to get another shot." Frankly I couldn't see how, but she was pretty good this one. Better than Moonbeam, that was for sure.

There was more but none of it was relevant to me.

After the cruise those of us who were kicking on went to Caroline's to change. She lives close to the city in a very groovy and sparse apartment. It looked rather like she and Teddy had a similar designer on board. Or maybe Caroline had gotten her ideas from Louisa's magazine. I hoped not.

Teddy caught me on the mobile phone between events as he was getting ready to go to the swanky work dinner at Fox Studios.

"I wish you were coming with me, baby."

"Well I have to be here with Lisa."

"I know, have fun and I'll call you in the morning. Miss you." And he was gone.

All day the girls had been a titter about Teddy. And all day I had been busy trying to divert their energy and attention to Lisa or the wedding, or just about anywhere.

I'm really just not comfortable being the centre of attention, as I told Caroline.

"Well that's what happens when you get mixed up with a celeb, baby." She was chopping strawberries for a batch of daiquiris. "Everyone wants a piece of you."

"Well, not when we're out together, then I'm totally invisible and everyone wants a piece of him."

"Weird conundrum", she shouted over the whirring blender.

It was indeed a weird conundrum.

We had a few drinks and some laughs and then ten of us hit a waterside restaurant at Circular Quay and then did a Rocks Pub crawl.

Lisa was having a lovely time and was completely blotto, as is the way of the Hen. I knew she'd be grateful, when sober, that Caroline and I managed to "misplace" that bridal veil one of her future sisters-in-law had wanted her to parade up Pitt Street wearing. Basically she would rather have gone naked down the street than worn it. We knew that. We'd even discussed the possibility in advance and a good thing too.

Lisa took me in an affectionate headlock about 1am to tell me she loved me, as all drunken brides do with their bridesmaids.

"I'll really miss you if you move to LA, but I still think you should do it."

"I'll keep that in mind."

"He's one of the good ones, you know?"

"I hope so."

***

Well by nine the next morning I was felt pretty sure we were completely wrong in our estimation.

Having not arrived home till sometime after 3am, I was none too excited to hear the phone when it began calling to me at 9am. I was even less thrilled to hear my mother, who had been totally avoiding me since the money handover day, on the other end.

"Allegra?"

"Yes," my weary voice probably not hiding my frustration.

"I thought you were dating that Teddy Green fellow."

"Yes, so?"

"Then how come his face is plastered across the newspaper this morning along with the announcement that last night he got engaged to some Louisa chick?"

She wasn't quite making sense. "What?"

"It says here in the paper that he and Louisa Lane got engaged and she is moving to LA with him. There are pictures of them leaving some TV shindig together last night. You're not very good at keeping track of your boyfriends, Allegra."

Ouch!

That was a clarifying life moment for me. I basically haven't had too many moments like it. I didn't know if I wanted to vomit, I certainly didn't know what the deal was with Teddy, and I didn't know for that brief second if I wanted to live or to die.

But I did know that my own mother shouldn't be relishing calling to tell me such a horrible thing. She had taken my last boyfriend and now she couldn't wait to be the one to take this one from me too.

"Good bye, Moonbeam." I hung up the phone and knew unequivocally, once and for-all, that I would never speak to her again. Despite the circumstances, it was an oddly freeing moment.

Then I went and vomited.

It was, I figured, the inevitable outcome of getting bad news after a night of cocktails, so why fight it?

When you feel wretched sometimes you retch.

A while later when I had peeled myself of the tiles, I went and woke Justin.

"Oh, my, you look disgusting; it must have been quite the hen event."

"It's not that' it's…"

Poor Justin had a hell of a time deciphering the situation between my sobs but, having worked it out, and announcing it must be just Machiavellian Moonbeam at her best, he raced down to get the morning papers.

When he came back and put the evidence before me, we were both speechless. And let me tell you that was a new state of being altogether for Juz.

"I don't understand, Ally."

"You don't understand? Imagine being me!"

"Precious, I can't even imagine." We had a huge hug and communal sob. "Has he called? He must have called, SMSed, something?" Justin located my phone which had an SMS and a voicemail saying, "call me", both around 6am.

"Call me, that's it? As if I'd be calling him. What a pig! What a mongrel!"

"He is an utter dog!" Agreed Juz.

"And I hate dogs, no wonder I hate them if this is how they behave."

"Frankly if this is how they behave, it's a wonder anyone likes them."

"Maybe they just have a bad rap?"

"Maybe. But you're getting off topic, Ally."

"I know."

We were sipping coffee by now.

By 10am my phone began ringing and Justin fielded calls from Lucie, Lisa and Caroline, none of whom I could bear to speak to.

Naturally, I was feeling beyond heartbroken. What is that expression about not really knowing what you've got till it's gone? I mean I had known Teddy was leaving to go away, but now that he had left me for Louisa no less, if he had ever really been with me at all, which frankly all made no sense, well now that he was gone I realised how I really felt about him.

Despite my best efforts, I'd fallen in love with the jerk. I felt so ridiculous. I felt insanely embarrassed. I felt a whole lot of things, really, and none of them were good.

Even Johno called, which was odd because he usually shies away from the more messy parts of my life. "I'm so sorry sweetheart. He seemed like a decent guy."

"Yes, he did. He fooled us all. I suppose that should make me feel better, knowing that I wasn't the only one suckered. But Dad, why did he even bother to pursue me? What was the point?"

"Maybe when you talk to him…"

"Talk to him! Are you insane? I'm never speaking to him again."

"I think you should, you need to know the deal. You'll need closure in a while."

"What is there to know? He's moving to LA next week and he's engaged to Louisa. Enough said. That's all the closure I need."

Justin and I decided the most appropriate course of action was for me to go back to bed and sleep off my hangover. Maybe without the throbbing headache, I'd have some clarity. And if nothing else, perhaps I would at least no longer have a throbbing headache.

When I re-emerged about 3pm after a nap and a long soak in the tub, my body felt clean and squeaky and revived, even if my soul was decidedly bruised.

Justin was flopped out on the couch watching sports. To know Justin is to know he didn't want to leave me alone, but must have been going out of his mind with boredom because sports are his worst nightmare.

"Feel a bit better now?"

"Yeah, a little."

"OK, well, the dashing yet dastardly Teddy Green called four times and is desperate to talk to you. He says he can explain." We both rolled our eyes in unison.

"What did you say?"

"I said you didn't want to talk to him."

"Which is true."

"He'll keep calling. He wasn't going to take no from me. That won't be enough."

"Did you try being all manly and scary?"

"He's met me, sweetie, that would have been rather pathetic and demeaned us both, don't you think?"

"True enough! You're watching motor racing, how bored are you?"

"Crazy bored. Insane bored. El polo loco bored."

"You're so bored you've lost the ability to make sense."

"Exactly, so let's go find some food with limited nutritional value and eat ourselves silly."

"Or we could go to Chinatown for noodles and duck."

"Even in your fragile state, Miss Allegra, you are a woman with wonderful ideas."

Or maybe I was just very hungry.

CHAPTER TWENTY

Justin pointed out that Teddy would probably show up that night at my place. Justin had had more than his fair share of dramatic and flamboyant break-ups so he knew the drill. I simply was not in the mood to deal with him. I was tired. I was confused. And I was mad as hell.

So, I did something highly indulgent and somewhat ridiculous under normal circumstances, but, as Justin kindly pointed out, circumstances were anything but normal.

So, with that in mind, I sent Justin home to man the fort and checked myself into a hotel.

And I didn't choose just any hotel either. I walked straight into a mega-expensive highly swanky five star hotel down by Circular Quay and booked a room. It's the kind of hotel where celebrities stay or people spend their wedding night and I just strolled in on a Sunday night, carrying nothing but my handbag, and booked myself a room with a spectacular view over Sydney Harbour. Can I tell you that it was a totally wonderful and liberating experience, aside from the fact I was drowning in misery.

I mean, women never do that stuff. Posh hotels are for romantic weekends away and business trips. It was so freeing to climb into the expansive marble bath and soak away my hangover and cares. You know you're in a bad way when you are on your second bath for the day by six o'clock.

I sat in the fluffy robe on the king-sized bed and painted my nails. I propped myself up on the thousands of pillows such hotels provide and ate a fantastic club sandwich from room service. I washed it down with a huge chocolate milkshake while watching the sappiest chick flick the in-house movies had to offer. I ate every last French fry on my plate and didn't feel the least bit guilty. I rolled around naked on the magnificent hotel sheets luxuriating in their sheer fabulousness and I almost felt pretty darn good by the time I fell asleep.

"I can take care of myself," I thought. "I don't need some guy to give me what I want!" That was liberating.

The next morning I ordered the big pancake breakfast and sat in the room watching the commuters get off the ferry and wind their way up to the CBD like tiny ants in a farm. The sun shone, the water sparkled and I thought,

"You'll be OK, Ally."

Justin arranged for Lucie to do the shop. I didn't ring him to find out if Teddy had stopped by. It didn't matter. I had the concierge call one of Sydney's most famous hairdressers and book me in for a cut. Concierges are great like that; they can always get you an appointment where you couldn't get one yourself.

While I was waiting, I took myself up to my favourite department store and strolled around looking at clothes. I bought a couple of very cute hairclips. I sat and had a huge cup of coffee and watched little old ladies meeting up for raisin toast and pots of tea nattering about movies, books and hip replacements.

I went into the hairdressers feeling good and made mindless chatter to the girl who did the wash. The fabulous hairdresser himself had a strange eastern European accent with a gay flourish that amused me greatly but made him almost incomprehensible. I just kept nodding and smiling. I wasn't sure if I would come out of there with a perm, a bob or as a blonde, but it didn't matter. In the end he gave me some layering and a trim and I basically just looked like a neater version of me, well until I washed it anyway.

When I finally got back home mid-afternoon, Teddy was sitting at the bottom of the stairs leading up to my flat. He looked rather dejected, but still amazingly cute. That seemed completely unfair to me, as I most definitely did not look cute. I looked like the hung-over, vomitty and dumped little thing that I was, even if I did now have fabulous hair and lots of over-flowing shopping bags.

And his dejection in no way altered the fact that had I not been a pacifist I would have murdered him with my bare hands.

He leapt up when he saw me. Justin must have seen me from in the shop because he immediately appeared behind me.

"Hey, Ally, uhmm hi, listen, well, uhmm I need to talk to you."

"I'm not interested".

"I need to explain."

"You don't. You don't owe me an explanation at all."

"I think I do."

"I think he does," Justin chimed in. He just wanted the gossip, we all knew that.

"Nobody cares what you think Justin. And Teddy you really don't need to explain. I wish you every success in the US and with your life. Now I'm really tired and I need to go inside so please move out of my way."

As I headed up the stairs he grabbed my arm "Ally! Look I'm not engaged to Louisa and…"

I turned and faced him down. I was glad I was a few stairs up; it gave me the powerful height advantage when I went to speak.

"Is that a 'not engaged with Louisa' in the same sense as you were at a work dinner, and not at dinner with HER Saturday night."

"I can explain that. It was just a work thing. It was arranged a long time ago."

"I doubt that, and even if it was, why didn't you just tell me? I was fine with her assaulting me and sending me to hospital, fine with her coming to my business, which is really my home, and threatening to steal you away. I was fine when her dog up-ended me in a water feature and I was even fine when you two wandered out for a romantic chat during the book launch after she was painfully rude to me and your folks. I was fine when all those things happened, or I should say, when you let all those things happen, when you did absolutely nothing to stop them or protect me from them. So seriously, Teddy, as if I would have had a meltdown over a simple dinner."

"But I just didn't want to create problems." And that, I thought, was Teddy Green to a tee, Mr Nice guy...

"Well, Teddy, it hasn't worked out that way. Now you are engaged to Louisa and for me, tolerant, ditzy door-mat of a gal that I clearly am, that is a big problem."

"I can fix it and again, for the record, I am not engaged to Louisa."

"Well the whole world thinks you are!" I turned to go and then turned back. "Either way, you can't fix it. And you know why? It's like snails in your cabbages, Teddy. You might get rid of the snails but there are still pesky little holes everywhere."

He stared at me. I stared at him. Justin stared at both of us.

I don't know what he felt but I felt a profound sadness. And then I walked up what felt like the world's longest staircase and went inside. It's a very long walk away from someone you love, even if you have no choice and even if it's only a few steps.

Justin obviously stayed to talk to him because I was already tucked up in bed with a book and a cup of tea by the time he flopped on my bed.

"Do you want to know what he says happened?"

"It won't make any difference to me."

"It might."

"It won't."

"What if I told you he was as surprised as you were to find out he was engaged today?"

"I'd say, that's crap!"

"Oh come on, Ally, let me at least tell you his version!"

"Can I go to sleep afterwards?"

"OK."

Justin's version of Teddy's tale was that, yes, he was at the dinner, and yes he knew Louisa was going, but they didn't go together. He says they walked out together and there were some reporters. He claims while he was talking to one, Louisa spoke to another. Apparently the gossip columnist asked Louisa if she and Teddy were back together and she said "Yes, and we are engaged!" Then someone snapped their picture. According to Justin, Teddy didn't know he was engaged till he started getting phone calls in the morning.

"That is a ridiculous and implausible tale, Justin!"

"But not impossible! That Louisa is highly manipulative."

"You are not seriously buying it are you?" I could not believe how quick he was to jump in and believe Teddy.

"Well if he was engaged to her why would he be here trying to make up with you so you'd move to LA with him? What would be the point, Ally?"

"Maybe he gets his jollies messing with people's heads?"

"Ally, you don't believe that!"

"Maybe I do. Anyway, I listened to you as promised, so now let me sleep."

"OK. He gave me this to pass to you."

"Maybe it's a bomb."

"Ally, you're just being ridiculous now. Open it."

Inside was an iPod. "Why would he give me an iPod?"

Justin took it out of the box and fiddled with it.

"Oh, Ally, how sweet, he's downloaded songs for you. This is like the twenty first century version of the classic mixed tape. It's full of mushy songs."

"Really?"

"Really? Now you can go to sleep listening to make-up music. Oh how cute, the first song is Deborah Conway's *It's Only the Beginning*."

"Not for me its not!"

"Listen to it, Ally, and go to sleep."

I did sleep for a little while and then I was up at 3am with that crazy insomniac racing brain that gets to gals in difficult situations such as mine.

I wondered if Teddy was up losing sleep too.

What Justin had told me sounded insane but then, as he had said, it wasn't technically impossible.

And if Teddy really were engaged to Louisa it didn't make sense that he would be over at my place trying to win me back. He would have been off having a wonderful day with her, calling his folks and sipping champagne with hers. If she had parents, I didn't know.

It occurred to me that I knew nothing about Louisa and Teddy, how long they'd been together or why they'd broken up. He had artfully avoided such questions in the past. He wasn't evasive in other matters, but he had not been forthcoming about Louisa. I did recall he had said she'd dumped him, but that was all the info I had.

Then a bizarre thought occurred to me. If they really were engaged, then they'd be together. She'd be at his place and they'd be snuggled up in bed together. If they weren't engaged, he'd be there on his own, hopefully pining over me.

At 4am I pulled on a pair of jeans and my favourite baby-blue cotton sweater and some flip-flops. I whipped my hair into a pony with a cute beaded hair tie and put on just enough concealer, foundation, mascara and lip-gloss to make me look human. A full-face of make-up at 4am seemed somewhat farcical, after all, but I didn't want to look too hideous whether Louisa was there or not.

I grabbed my keys, left Justin a note and headed out to the van. Driving over the Spit Bridge and Middle Harbour was really quite beautiful. The sun was beginning to do a lazy wriggle and get up, as it tends to do late in summer.

I hoped today would be a better day for me than yesterday.

Worst-case scenario was he was there with Louisa and I looked like a mild psycho. Best-case scenario was he was there alone, and I would know he wasn't a total liar, and I'd still probably look like a psycho.

Whether I was willing to forgive him or not for screwing up and not fully getting rid of Louisa, I couldn't say.

As I pulled up outside Teddy's place and parked the Kombi, I had no idea how it would play out.

I wanted to forgive him, if only so we could part on good terms. I hate bad blood, that's the thing with being a people pleaser like me; you want even complete bastards to like you.

I supposed that maybe that was Teddy's problem with Louisa, he wanted it over, but he didn't want to be the bad guy. Well, even if that was so, that was his problem not mine.

I knocked on his front door with my heart in my mouth, wearing my heart on my sleeve and of course with my heart pounding. How could one heart be in so many places at once?

CHAPTER TWENTY-ONE

A disheveled looking Teddy answered the front door. Who doesn't look disheveled at that hour? To say he looked surprised to see me would be an understatement. His surprise was a happy, one I thought, rather than an oh-no-bugger-this one.

"Hey, Ally", he ran his fingers through his hair, "what brings you here?"

"I know it sounds kind or weird but I just wanted to see if you had company."

"Oh baby, you do care!" He gave me that big broad, engaging, to-die-for grin.

"Don't get excited buddy, this is about resolution not restitution."

"Baby, its 5am and I don't even know what that means. How about you come in and search the premises while I turn on the coffee machine."

"OK." It sounded like a fair deal and I was totally stinging for a coffee.

I went through his house room by room. With each room I searched I felt more unhinged. It just didn't feel right. I felt like I was being lowered to a level I had never wanted to reach, that my search was demeaning us both.

When I returned downstairs the smell of coffee was overwhelming and Teddy looked so earnest and contrite, though I must admit a little too sure of himself for my liking, but still, extraordinarily cute.

"Anything interesting up there you want to report on?"

"Well, I did find two bedrooms I hadn't seen before. Though I must tell you from a design perspective they were a little too sterile and not that welcoming!"

"But no freaky ex-girlfriends."

"Apart from myself?"

"Well, I didn't exactly have you in that category but yes, apart from you?"

"Nope, no one, else."

"Cool. Pull up a sofa and have a coffee."

We lay on different sofas on opposite sides of his spartan back room and sipped our coffee. I don't know how long we were there exactly. Almost morning became actual morning, and I felt more and more settled as the time passed.

OK, so there was no Louisa, that was a good thing, but still he had some explaining to do. Maybe I have deep-seated issues that prevented me from delving deeper at that moment, or maybe I just like a companionable silence, which knows?

It was Teddy who broke the silence with the cataclysmic question, "Can I get you another coffee?"

"Sure."

"So, Ally, if you get a morning paper today you will read the headline 'Louisa Lies - she and Teddy never engaged'."

"Will she be OK?"

"Do you really care baby?" He was back in baby mode again.

"Actually, not really."

"Fair enough." He handed me a frothy coffee.

"Anything you want to tell me?"

"Can I start with I'm sorry?"

"It's never a bad place…" Well he did owe me apology.

"Look you would not believe the stuff that has rained down on me in the past 24 hours; I mean from my dad alone, it was like too much."

"Sorry."

"No, but it was cool. I let the Louisa stuff slide too long. I thought I was making it easier on her, and me, but it was a disaster. We broke up because she has some issues. Well we had some issues too, I guess."

"What kind?"

"No. That was one of the issues. She said she never wanted kids, and I did.

Anyway, I thought she would get it in time and understand that for me that was non-negotiable, but it didn't happen that way. She wanted what she wanted the lifestyle and being part of 'us' and she wasn't going to step away graciously."

"No kidding! It took the engagement to figure that out?"

"No not exactly but, I don't like to assume the worst in people. She wasn't always like this. At her core I know the excellent bits I liked in the start still linger."

"OK, I'll take your word for it." You had to like a guy who saw the best even in the most hideous of people.

"Look I mismanaged it and I hurt you, I can't take that back."

"No, you can't." I sipped my coffee like it would give me courage. "I have a question?"

"Sure"

"I just don't understand why you and Louisa were ever together, or why you were together so long."

"Yes, well, that's complicated. The short answer is habit from my side anyway and optimism."

"You were together ten years out of habit?"

"Kind of. First it was fun. Then I think she got sick of me but the TV thing happened. Then I was sick of her but she had gotten me the gig. Then we were like 'the couple' and then we'd been together so long…it's not like it was all bad."

"I suppose."

"Look around, Ally, when you watch people there are couples bonded by love and couples bonded by economy or family but so many are together because neither of them quite has the courage or the conviction to break free. You must know people like that?"

"Maybe…."I couldn't off the top of my head think of any but that made sense at least.

"You don't hate the other person, you even quite like them, and you know they'd be great for someone else, but you don't know how to break free? With us we both tried to break it off at different times but the other person resisted…"

"That's kind of sad, to think there are people living like that all over. Yes and what was the optimism part?"

"Oh that's easy. We had so much fun when we first got together. The optimism is believing you can get back to that place again and that the relationship will go the way you planned for it to go in the first place."

I nodded. That was easy to understand. Kind of like I wished our relationship could be the way it was a few days earlier, even though I was a whole lot less optimistic we could make that happen.

He crossed the room and sat next to me on the couch and took my hand." But Ally out of all this what I have learnt is the difference between that and the real thing. I love you and really to me that is what matters."

He'd never said he loved me before, he'd said "falling in love" but not actual love. What was I to do with that new and rather fabulous, though disconcerting information? Nothing of course. I'd simply pretend he had never said it.

"Can I get another latte, perhaps?" I asked.

"Sure."

"So what happens now, Ally?"

"I don't know. You go to LA next weekend that is all that seems clear to me right now."

"OK."

It was coming up for 9am. I had to be in to open the shop at 10am, time to go.

"Can I see you tonight? So we can talk about it?"

"I may be too tired for much. I don't normally get up at 3am."

"OK, we'll I'll take you for a pizza. There's never a bad time to go for pizza." How could I argue with logic like that? There really never is a bad time to go for pizza.

It was a long day with another round of phone calls from everyone I knew. On days like these I was quite glad I didn't have a larger circle of friends to deal with. The consensus seemed to be universal: that Teddy had fixed everything.

Of course Lucie and Justin had the newspapers long before I arrived.

"Well he has redeemed himself, Ally." Justin was always quick with an opinion.

"I suppose so."

"He has," conferred Lucie.

"Of course he has!" Justin was emphatic. "I wouldn't want to be Louisa. That is very humiliating to be announced both a liar and dumped on the front page of the paper."

"Well, Justin, she did bring it on herself." Lucie was obviously not in a compassionate mood.

Justin spent the first half the morning hanging out in the shop. Then he flitted off to meet his editors and discuss his next freelance assignment. He returned late afternoon to announce he was off to Russia the following week to work on a guidebook.

"Won't it be freezing there?"

"Sweetie, it is eternally freezing there."

I left the shop at 4pm for a much needed nap. I didn't want to look quite so dreadful when Teddy came to take me for dinner.

Teddy arrived with yet another expansive and decadent bunch of flowers.

"You really didn't need to do that."

"I know but they were beautiful and they reminded me of you."

"Flattery is the theme of the evening is it?"

"Maybe," he grinned

"OK, well, there are worse themes."

We walked around the corner to my favourite pizza joint. It's not on the water, like so many of the restaurants in Manly, but it's intimate and makes great pizza. All the menus are written on surfboards, but the walls are dark, the music is low and every table has a candle. Barney, who runs it, is an old friend, in as much as I'm a regular.

"Hey, Ally, Table for two?"

"Thanks Barney. Oh, this is Teddy. Teddy meet Barney, Barney meet Teddy." They did the handshake thing.

"You know people everywhere, baby." He said as we were being seated.

"Only in my neighbourhood."

"Someone as friendly as you will have no problem meeting new people in LA."

"Teddy! You're crazy."

"I still really want you to come. You know, the only good thing about the newspaper debacle was that it showed me how much I really don't want to lose you."

"I feel the same way."

"That's the first time you've really said that." He said giving my hand a hard squeeze.

We were interrupted when Barney came with the wine.

The fact that we were huddled in close over the table holding hands was no doubt highly amusing for Barney and everyone else in that restaurant who had read a paper in the past 24 hours. We certainly were getting some quizzical looks. I had expected as much and had dressed up in some black pants, a cute floral chiffon top over a singlet and some sparkly shoes. I had just one small, diamante hair slide keeping my hair tucked behind my right ear.

Teddy was quickly back on topic, clearly oblivious to the stares.

"I'm glad you really want to be with me, too."

"Sure, but that doesn't mean I'm up for relocation, Teddy. I mean what would I do there? I can't just sit around all day on my own."

"True. OK, what have you always wanted to do?"

"Apart from go to Disneyland?"

"Yes apart from that, which we will do as many times as you like." He was massaging my fingers seductively so frankly a whole life plan was hard to formulate right then.

"Well, I've always wanted to design my own jewellery and hair accessories, which by the way is totally ridiculous."

"Well you could study jewellery design there, surely. They love jewellery in

LA don't they?" He made a good point. "Plus it would give you the opportunity to do that, you know, make you take the plunge. And you'd meet lots of people that way too."

"Teddy, you're being ridiculous. I would have to get accepted into a course and get a study visa. It would cost a fortune."

"Is that really an issue – the money I mean? And the other things, they can be sorted out." Maybe they could be. And he was right about the money, it really wasn't an issue. "Look I'm not suggesting you come on Sunday to stay forever. But think about making the move. Now enough of that let's just relax and have fun."

The pizza arrived and it was amazingly good. I was a bit exhausted and the red wine gave me a warm glowing feeling.

Teddy loved me and Louisa was off the scene.

The one question I still kept asking myself was "Why did Teddy love me?"

CHAPTER TWENTY-TWO

Tuesday

Teddy left my place early in the morning to go and deal with a million aspects of his move.

"Just think about LA, Allegra. It could be a wonderful adventure."

On the advice of the lovely Lisa, who met me for a coffee and post-hen's day and pre-wedding update on Tuesday morning, I decided to immerse myself in Teddy and his life.

It was most convenient she was having the week off to prepare for her wedding.

"How will you know what you're giving up otherwise? And you may as well enjoy him while you have got him, Ally."

So I decided to copy Lisa and take the week off myself between final dress fittings and wedding activities, had I been working full time I wouldn't have even seen Teddy. Deb and Lucie were more than happy to take up the slack.

"Go! Enjoy! You are completely mad if you don't," Deb said almost pushing me out the shop door.

That night was dinner with Teddy's parents and younger brother Rory, who came down for a farewell. Rory was like the totally laddish version of Teddy. He was a highly rakish and affable twenty-one year old who liked rugby, beer and girls in that exact order. Bob and Joyce were as sweet as can be.

"So, Teddy tells us you grew up on communes, dear. That must have been very interesting. Our boys have led such mundane lives, comparatively."

"I wouldn't say that dear…"

They were really excited for Teddy and their enthusiasm was infectious.

"Well Teddy's life is about to get a whole lot more exciting with the big move."

"Yes, Ted, have you started packing, or will they kit you out on new clothes over there?"

"I think they will Mum, but I am sure I'll still need to take my own things too."

"It's hard to believe. I remember when you started that first little veggie garden at age five. Who knew it would lead you all the way to Los Angeles? Do you need me to help you pack dear?"

"I think I can manage Mum."

"Well the whole thing is just amazing!" She shook her head as if she couldn't still quite believe it.

Wednesday

The day began with breakfast with the Green clan. It was kind of weird walking down the stairs and seeing Bob and Joyce their reading *Sydney Morning Herald*. Teddy was on the phone finalizing his day.

"Oh good morning, sweetheart! Don't you look lovely" OK breakfast with Joyce was good weird, not bad weird. "I'm about to make omelettes, would you like one?"

"That would be lovely!" And it was. I wasn't used to the sort of mum who rose from the table to greet you and whisk some eggs.

"So Ally, I wanted to go in to the city and do some shopping today. Would you care to join me? Not if you have plans of course."

"I have to collect my bridesmaid dress for this weekend's wedding at three, but I'm all yours till then."

"Terrific," said Teddy. "My two favourite girls spending the day together. OK

I'm off. I have to go in to the station and film some promos. I'll meet you back here at six for dinner as planned Ally."

Shopping with Joyce was totally fun. She talked non-stop. Touched every dress she even vaguely liked, checking the seams and cut of the fabric.

"I'm happy to pay for quality, Allegra, but this isn't it!" It was a riot.

In the end she bought herself some new shoes and several shirts for Teddy.

"I know he wouldn't want anyone to know his mother still dresses him, but we can't have him going off to America looking shabby now, can we?"

She insisted we have lunch at the department store café.

"I always eat here Ally. It's a tradition. It drives Bob nuts of course. But then he isn't here," she grinned and gave my hand a conspiratorial pat.

It was such a fun day I was sorry to tear myself away to go to the dress fitting.

"We'll have to do this in LA dear."

"I'm not sure I'm going to LA, Joyce."

"I know sweetie, it is a very big decision. I hope you do, because I know Teddy has very strong feelings for you, and you're good for each other, but no one will hold it against you if you don't."

No wonder Teddy was so amazing, I thought, heading off on the bus, he took after his parents.

That night was a farewell at a pub with his colleagues from work. No doubt a celebrity spotter's paradise but the only faces I recognised were Janie and a few from my day on the set. Janie had her husband, Glen, with her.

"So nice to meet you Allegra. Janie has told me so much about you."

"Nothing too horrific, I hope."

"Only good things," he smiled. I decided to sit down next to him and chat while Teddy worked the room." We'll miss Ted. He and Janie are great friends, been together a long time."

"I'm sure that won't change."

"Oh no, but you know, it's not the same as seeing someone every day."

He was certainly right about that.

It turned into quite a party and with everyone buying him drinks Teddy was quite tipsy by the time the pub closed.

"I'm really going to miss those people", he said as I helped him into the back of a taxi and slid in beside him. "It takes time to make good friends like that."

"It certainly does."

"I hope I'm not too lonely over there. Will be very lonely if you don't come... Really hope you come." he mumbled before nodding off on my shoulder.

Thursday

Thursday needless to say, started slowly. Joyce and Bob were nowhere to be seen when we finally emerged.

There was just a note saying – You two need some privacy. See you later. Mum.

"That's a bit embarrassing," I said.

"Yeah especially as I need aspirin a lot more than privacy right now."

"So many parties, so little time."

"You got that right," he said throwing back the tablets as he sat down at the table. "This week is going way to fast. I feel like there are a million things to do and not enough time by half."

"I know. You can skip the wedding if it all gets too hard. Lisa will understand."

He pulled me onto his lap and hugged me hard. "Baby, I will not be skipping anything where I get to spend time with you."

"That's very sweet, but if you have to, you have to."

He gave me a long hard kiss. "I will not have to, OK?"

"OK."

"Feel like making the most of that privacy?"

"I could be persuaded," I replied returning his kiss.

Thursday night was dinner with Teddy's mates at a very trendy Thai restaurant in Sydney's east. It was one of those themed places where we all sat on cushions and the table was low to the floor. His friends all seemed very sweet and most had delightful girlfriends. Only Guy, the dude, was single. Most of his friends I vaguely recognised from Teddy's housewarming, where I had wrongly assumed that they all rotated through their girlfriends. Nothing could have been further from the truth. Most, in fact, were married and some even had small kids. I'm sure they all had varying degrees of connection with Louisa but they were all way too polite to bring that up.

Teddy seemed particularly interested in all their children, asking copious questions about their progress.

In the restroom, where many of the key conversations of my life seem to occur, one girl, Julia, took me aside.

"We're all so glad to meet you properly at last. I hope you do go with Teddy, to LA."

"Well, I'm not sure about that."

"I wouldn't leave him over there alone too long. He is completely adorable; one of those American women will snap him up fast."

She made a good point.

"He loves kids, Teddy. Do you like kids?"

"Uhm yes." Not that it was any of her business frankly.

"That's good. I know Teddy wants a big family."

"Oh?" This girl was moving way to fast for me.

"Yes, at least three or four kids. Do you come from a big family?"

"Well I'm one of six actually!" When you added in all my half sisters and brothers I was. Not that I had ever lived with any of them.

"Oh well, you'll understand the attraction then."

Well I did but not for the reasons she thought. Imagine being part of a family or even a mother of three or four kids. I had never really even let my mind go there. I think my fear of being as appalling a mother as Moonbeam always stopped me in my tracks.

That night back at Teddy's we had a post-mortem of the evening in the pool.

"You seemed to get along with everyone really well, baby."

"Everyone was very friendly. Lots of them have kids."

"It's that time of life."

"Apparently you want six kids."

He blinked hard, "Who told you that?"

"A little bird." Hey I didn't want to dob anyone in.

"A little bird called Julia, perhaps?"

"Perhaps."

"A bit too much information for you huh?"

"I don't even know what's happening with us now, so yeah a little much to digest."

"Well hypothetically, where are you on big families?" he asked lifting my foot out of the water to give me one of his incredible massages.

"Well hypothetically, I'm fine with them but I think I'd take it on a kid-by-kid basis." I was hardly going to deny the man his hypothetical children while he was massaging my foot.

"OK. Fair enough." He said as his hand began to massage further up my leg.

"Teddy, your parents are upstairs."

"Don't worry they're sound sleepers."

I certainly hoped he was right!

Friday

Time to head home and get into the pre-wedding excitement. And after several days away I also needed clean clothes and some time to think. Mid-morning I stood in the bookshop and remembered my time there.

The shop's bell tinkled, which it does often, as you now know, and Justin was standing behind me in the doorway.

"So, Ally, what are you going to do?"

"I have no idea," I wailed.

"Sweetie this is not a tragedy you know. A cute guy wants you to move across the world and be with him. You like the guy and he seems genuine. Hard though it is for you to believe, most people would be quite happy about now."

"Well, I'm not most people, Juz."

"Clearly." Sigh. "OK tell me what the main sticking points are."

Really there was only one main sticking point. In order to go, I had to leave.

"Ally, do you intend to sit here in this shop your entire life?"

"I don't know. I had sort of thought so."

"Why?"

"Why? What do you mean why? Because it's my home."

"And why else?"

"And because I love it."

"More than Teddy?"

"Well I've loved it longer, at least."

"Well how can you love him longer if you never give him the chance?" That was a pretty fair question.

"Why do I have to move to love him? Who says his career is more important than mine anyway?"

"Ally, nobody says that. It's simply that he has to do this NOW, there won't be another chance for him."

"Justin, it's a big move to make with someone you've only known a month, surely you can see that..."

"Sure, but do you want to look back and wish you'd done it, when he is gone?"

"I don't know!"

Justin was starting to talk to me as if I was a petulant child. That was starting to bug me, frankly. "Listen Ally, it's your decision but I want you to think about it hard. Didn't you tell me this shop was your grandma's plan B, that when she thought she couldn't have kids she opened the shop?"

"So?"

"So why is it your plan A? Why don't you have your own plan? Why did you so readily put your own life and plans on hold when you were left this shop?"

I really hadn't ever thought of it quite like that.

"I guess I just wanted to be close to her and do the right thing by her, like she did by me."

"What about doing the right thing by YOU? Nancy would have wanted that." He was right. She always wanted the very best for me. "Ally, you don't have to be either Moonbeam or grandma…you can be just you. The one thing that our hippie parents got right was that people need freedom to choose their own life. So why not choose a great brave exciting life."

"What if I'm not a great, brave, exciting person?" I certainly didn't feel like one.

"What if you are? Did you ever think that? What if you are?"

Teddy stopped by for a late dinner. He was busy packing and getting ready to fly out on Sunday.

He looked quite tired poor thing, but he smelt lovely as always. I guess it had been a stressful week for him too, what with promoting the book, finishing the show and downplaying the fake engagement and of course the whole relocation issue.

Dinner was just a veggie frittata. You don't want to be trying to digest too much that late in the day.

Neither of us was particularly chatty, because I guess by then we'd said all we could.

He had made all his persuasive arguments and I had avoided giving him an answer.

As he snuggled down next to me in bed I wondered if this might be the last snuggling I did with Teddy.

About 3am I woke him up for a chat.

"Are you asleep?"

"Not really."

"Liar! You were snoring."

"Well, why ask then? What can I do for you?" Total guy, wakes up raring to go, hands wandering.

"No, not that just now, I don't want you to do THAT thanks very much. Though maybe in a few minutes," he had persuasive hand. "I have to ask you something."

"Sure baby, anything." He sat up, put his hands behind head and nestled in the pillows.

"Why me?"

"Sorry?"

"Why me? Why do you like me? Look at you, you're mister big shot, you're mister man-of-the-moment, you're the guy everyone wants...so why do you want me?"

"Are you serious?" He looked so solemn.

"Deadly. I just don't get it. You bump into me on a street and then boom, it has to be me. It doesn't make sense."

"Baby, you're the only one it doesn't make sense to. It's called love and what everyone else already knows is that it never makes any sense at all."

"Huh?"

"Look, I think you are totally amazing and the most incredible, interesting, sexy person I've ever met in my entire life. Don't you get that?"

"Kind of... but, no, not really."

"Well that's love. Whoever you love is everything to YOU, even if no one else gets it and the person you love doesn't even have to get it. It just is. It's random. For me you are the right one. You are it. "

"But what if you're wrong?"

"There's no wrong. You can't get it wrong. You love someone and you hope they love you. And even if they don't you weren't wrong, you were unlucky."

"Well I feel it. I mean, I do love you."

"Well there you have it." He kissed me slowly. "You just have to trust it."

But could I? How could I trust it?

***

I was up and gone by 6am for the whole pre-wedding make-up, hair and champagne ritual.

I couldn't believe how calm Lisa was. I expected her to be the wreck that all brides are meant to be.

"It's the weirdest thing. I woke up and I just thought 'today I am getting married'. It made me feel so amazing. I get to be with him every day from now on. It just made me feel so centred."

When we were all dressed up having our photos taken I couldn't help but comment on how different we were from that first day I'd met them at FernHill.

"I don't really think we are," said Caroline. "Oh of course we look infinitely better out of those hideous uniforms but we are the same people. We are who we were then; kind one, the brave one and the searcher. And let's face it, we all knew then as we know now, which one is us."

Maybe she was right. I was the searcher then, searching for a home which I found, maybe I was searching now for something more. The question I asked myself as I over-smiled for the photos was "Had I found that something in Teddy?"

CHAPTER TWENTY-THREE

The ceremony was gorgeous and the reception was divine. It seemed to me to be everything Lisa and her mum had envisaged.

The restaurant sat over the water, which in turn sparkled fantastically as if on cue. The champagne flowed. You could feel the love in the room. It was palpable.

I was sitting with Teddy, after all the speeches, as the band began.

"So it seems to me, Allegra, you have a decision to make." Teddy held my hands tight and looked at me with his twinkling blue eyes. How could I possibly make a decision right here, right now? "Meanwhile, baby, how about we dance?"

"Really?"

"Really! After all we are at a wedding and there is a band playing."

"OK". So it was that simple, I did have to make a decision, but not right now. In the meantime I could keep on dancing.

As we hit the dance floor where the band was doing a cover of an upbeat Van Morrison song and shifted gears into Norah Jones *Come away with me*. Could that be a sign?

Teddy laughed, "I paid them to play that."

"Really?"

"No, not really." He pulled me in close as he shook his head at how gullible I was.

All around me the people I cared about were dancing and happy. And with

Teddy's arms around me I felt happy too, not freaked out anymore. It was strange because I am not much of a dancer and Teddy and I had never danced together but it just seemed right.

The song changed again. He swung me out and then whoosh pulled me back in again. He held me close again.

I thought about that feeling. That warmth and extreme closeness.

I thought about not having that anymore. About him not being here anymore. And I didn't like the thought of me still being here without him.

I looked up at him as the song ended and smiled.

"Teddy."

"Yes baby."

"I've made my decision…"

THE END

Acknowledgements

This book has been a labour of love for some years. I have many people to thank for their encouragement, support and input. Of course I must thank my lovely husband , Ross and my gorgeous daughter Charlotte for believing in me, supporting me and cheering me on. Thanks also to my many friends and relatives who have anxiously followed my path to publication and shown such interest and enthusiasm for my efforts.

Special thanks to the wonderful members of The Writers' Dozen who have supported this book since its first day. Special thanks must go to Deborah Green and Jules Jones who were my earliest readers and to Pam Cook, Angella Whitton, Jen Tomasetti, Pauline Reynolds and Yvonne Louis who have been my eternal cheer squad.

A huge thank you also goes to the Joondi 8 for their ongoing encouragement, and to Ber Carroll, Deanna Hathorne and Linda Gauthier for all their input. Finally thanks to Jacqui Fishpool who helped me get this project over the line in 2012.

About the author

I am an Australian author who writes contemporary women's fiction including chick lit and romance. I live on Sydney's Northern Beaches with my husband and daughter, and despite my dog phobia, with a dog called Skip.

I have written all my life especially as a child when I loved to write short stories and poetry. At University I studied Creative Writing as part of my Communication degree. After wards I was busy working in public relations I didn't write for pleasure for quite a few years although I wrote many media releases, brochures and newsletters. (And I still do in my day-job!)

When I began to write again I noticed a trend - writing dark unhappy stories made me unhappy. So I made a decision to write a novel with a happy ending and I have been writing happy stories ever since. I began a year-long writing course at the NSW Writers Centre and (thank goodness) its members morphed into a writing group known as The Writer's Dozen. We published a highly successful anthology, Better than Chocolate, in 2008.

In 2008 I was also selected for the QWC/Hachette Livre Manuscript Development Course for my novel Mr Right and Other Mongrels. In 2009 I received a Highly Commended in the Romance Writers of Australia's Valerie Parv Awards for my novel Hearts Afire.

These are the first two books I will be e-publishing in 2012 along with a third novel, A Fair Exchange. I'm not really like the characters in my books at all although I do share something in common with each of them - Allegra (Mr Right and Other Mongrels) has a dog phobia like me, Cassie (Hearts Afire) falls in love on a tropical island and I met my husband that way and Amelia (A Fair Exchange) was an exchange student who is now all grown up.

To learn more about Monique McDonell and her upcoming books please visit her at www.moniquemcdonell.com.au.

www.ingramcontent.com/pod-product-compliance
Lightning Source LLC
Chambersburg PA
CBHW071355250626
47159CB00004B/1629

* 9 780987 330802 *